In with the Tide

In with the Tide

A Cape Cod Shore Novel

Charlee James

TULE
PUBLISHING

Dedication

For Mom and Dad, my personal cheerleading team.
Thanks for all of those wonderful Cape Cod memories.

Acknowledgements

Thank you to the Tule Publishing Team, it has been a pleasure to work with you. Special thanks to Sinclair, Michelle, and Meghan for their dedication, support, and late-night emails.

To Darcy, who left a permanent imprint on my heart, your love and sweetness will never be forgotten.

Chapter One

DAMIEN'S BIKE ROARED inland, the salt water wind whipping at his face. His father was dead. He had tried to feel something—anything—when he had received the phone call, but all he could muster was the numb realization that he was truly alone. The last blood tie, the final rope tying him to his past, severed.

His stomach clenched when he passed the dirt drive that led to his childhood home. It was miles from downtown, with a driveway that snaked toward a rundown Cape house. He could still feel the sharp bite of a belt licking his vulnerable skin, still smell the cheap alcohol curtaining the stale air. He ordered his mind to go blank, a trick he learned in the Marines to cool his nerves when shells exploded into the ground around him. Damien wanted to get into town, rent a room for the night, and fall into a dreamless sleep. He knew the latter wouldn't happen, not with shadows and ghosts lurking around every corner and the funeral looming only days ahead.

He was thinking of stopping at Clancy's for a bite and grabbing a six-pack from the convenience store when he rounded the bend, squeezed his hand over the grip, and came to a skidding halt. The small sedan was broken down in the worst possible spot—a bend in a blind drive. White smoke clouded the air around it. The driver stood on the side of the road, back turned to him, a thick fall of wheat-colored hair cascading over her shoulders. Damien forgot to breathe. Another ghost.

Lindsey Hunter turned toward him. It was as though someone landed a one-two punch square in his gut. He couldn't move, couldn't think. The familiar green eyes that matched the pines lining the roadway shot him a wary glance. The message was clear. *Stay back.* She didn't remember him as he had her. And why would she? He was just the scrubby kid on the school bus with second-hand clothes. The kid that tried to steal the contents of her lunch box when it had fallen under the seat.

She'd caught him, gripped his wrists with surprising ferocity for a young kid, and asked him why. He wasn't sure why he told her the truth; lies had spilled off his tongue like water for everyone else. She might not recall the extra peanut butter sandwich she carried in the metal Barbie box after that day, but he'd never forget it. Those two slices of bread slapped together with spread oozing out the sides might have seemed like a small gesture to some, but at the time it had been everything to him.

"You don't have to stop." Her jaw was set and her shoulders squared, but she stepped back. "I already called roadside assistance."

Damien stood, swung his leg over the bike, and kicked the stand out. "There's no cell signal on this road. Never has been." He walked over and took a glance under the hood of the car. "When's the last time you replaced the fluids in this thing?"

When he looked up at her, he was surprised to see the heavily rounded belly, and understood the caution that clouded her eyes. Voice softer now, he met her eyes. "Lindsey. Don't you remember me?"

She paused a moment, and then recognition replaced the caution. She put a hand over her heart and let out a big sigh of relief before rushing forward. Lindsey swung her arms around his shoulders and he gave her back a quick pat. He hadn't had much physical contact—in a pleasant way—during his time in Afghanistan.

"I'm so sorry, Damien. I didn't recognize you. You've buzzed off all that hair, but the eyes are still the same coastal-blue." She smiled at him now. "I should have known." She puffed out another breath. "Pregnancy hormones have me on edge."

"When?" he asked and looked back under the hood.

"Won't be much longer now. My due date is August twelfth." She rested a hand over her belly. By the looks of things, she wasn't going to make it to the due date, but he kept his mouth shut.

"One month left. Congratulations." She was as beautiful

3

now as she was then, standing before him with a warm glow blushed over her face. Pregnancy looked good on her, as had everything else.

"You can't just sit on the road. This thing's not going to start up again on its own."

She pressed a hand to her forehead. "I know you're right about the car. About the cell signal. I just don't want to leave everything, and my dog is in the front seat."

He lowered the hood and sure enough a black-and-white dog with a flat face, bulging eyes, and pointed ears too big for its head stared inquisitively back at him.

"A dog or a bat?" he questioned. "Pop the trunk. I'll get what you have and drive you and the bat into town."

She bit her full bottom lip and sent a nervous glance toward the bike.

"I'll go slow." Driving her would put a wrench in his plans, but there was no way he'd leave her stranded—or the dog, if you could call it that. He glanced at her and his heart thumped faster. He'd never been immune to Lindsey.

"I'm not sure it's safe in my current state, and with Daisy." She put a protective hand over her belly.

"What choice do you have?" Damien rounded the car to the passenger side and opened the door. The dog was sitting contently in a little canvas tote, which was strapped around the headrest, hoisting it up for a perfect view of the road. He shook his head and a grin stretched over his face. The things people did for their pets. "Is the bat in a car seat?"

Lindsey laughed. "It's a booster seat. She likes to look out the window, but she's too short."

"You're in for a rude awakening when that baby comes," Damien said to the dog. He ran his hand over its head, and the dog turned its snout to lap its tongue over his palm. "You and your booster seat can sit right on the bike." Damien lifted the dog out and started tying the booster to his bike.

Lindsey rounded the car, poked into the driver's side, and popped the trunk. It was a wonder it hadn't busted open on its own.

"Planning on staying long?" His brows popped up when a bag sprang out of the over-packed car. Was she running from something?

"I never should have left." He could read between the lines. She didn't wear a ring, not that it meant anything, but no man with a spine would let the mother of his child-to-be take a road trip alone—especially with the due date looming so close. "I'm putting down roots," she said now, voice fiercer. "What about you? You only have a backpack."

"I'm pulling them up. I won't be staying long." Was that disappointment that flashed over her face, or the heat and smog from the highway tricking his eyes and fogging his mind?

"Do you have a pack of essentials? We can take what you need into town, call the tow service, and get the rest when it pulls into the shop."

She nodded. "I'll just need a second to sort through." He watched her retrieve a purse from the front seat and a small duffel from the back, and thought of how appealing she looked in the long breezy skirt and simple white tee. He had no business thinking of her that way—pregnant and all. Just as he had no business thinking of her in grade school. She had been honor roll and pom-poms. He had been torn jeans, leather jackets, and trouble.

"Okay, I think that's all the necessities." She struggled with the zipper until it finally closed. It would be a challenge to ride with the overstuffed bag, but he'd make it work. Damien opened the left saddlebag and stowed her purse.

"Put this on." He shifted and handed her his helmet. Her long silky hair flowed over full breasts. He swallowed and looked away.

She clipped the helmet straps under her chin and held his shoulders for balance as she slowly—and very awkwardly—mounted the bike.

"Now hang on real tight," he called over the roar of the engine springing to life. She listened. Her arms wound tight around his waist, gripping on like he was the last life preserver on a sinking ship. Lindsey's scent, something sweet and warm, teased his senses and made his stomach grip. Her belly bump pressed against his back, reminding him to ignore his visceral reactions.

He had enjoyed women through the years, but they never stuck—or he never let them. He was smart enough to know he wasn't his father, but not naive enough to forget they were of the same gene pool. Damien wasn't sure if he was cut from the kind of cloth that wrapped itself up in a relationship, one where the threads grew stronger over time instead of fraying. It was the same reason he allowed himself a beer or two, but never drank to excess. He wasn't an addict like his father, but never forgot he came from one, either.

He drove more slowly than he ever had, avoiding potholes as if they were sinkholes in the road. The dog seemed to be enjoying the journey, as it sat in front of him on the bike. Her head was tilted to the sky and her nose wrinkled as she sniffed the scents that tangled in the breeze. Lindsey on the other hand, had a tight hold on his waist and didn't loosen it until they pulled into a parking space in front of John's Tire Shop and Road Side Assistance.

"Thanks for the lift. Under different circumstances, I think I would have really enjoyed it." She smiled a little now, and lifted the saddlebag for her purse.

Her face was just as he remembered, so fresh and pretty. Damien was faced with a moral dilemma. Should he leave her? Let her sort this out on her own?

He couldn't help himself. "Who are you staying with?" he asked, and took the helmet she handed back to him.

"Myself—and Daisy. I purchased the cottage on the shore." She smoothed her hands over her skirt and unclipped the dog from the booster. "A place to start fresh," she added. "Do you remember Mrs. McFee's old place? That's the one."

"Yeah, I remember it." He also remembered it was in a remote area, with no other homes for miles and miles and Daisy was the furthest thing from a watch dog. "What about your folks? They still in town?"

"Time-share in Aruba." Lindsey turned away from him and walked to the door of the shop. "They'll be back closer to my due date."

A heavy weight of responsibility rested upon Damien's shoulders. One for the perfect little girl he once knew, and one for the woman he was standing with now.

"Okay then, let's get the car towed." A cold beer and solitude seemed a long way off but this was Lindsey.

"Damien, I appreciate your help, but you don't have to wait." She brushed a strip of hair off her face. She must be dying in this heat.

"By the time John gets back with the car, it'll be almost dusk. When he fixes it—if he can fix it today—it will be dark before you get to the cottage." By the look on her face, he knew he'd hit a mark. She may be independent, but she wasn't stupid. "You should get a room in town. Wait until morning to open up the cottage." He shoved his hands into his jean pockets.

Lindsey sighed. "You seem to be the voice of reason today. As much as I want to get to the cottage, I don't know what condition it's in or what type of cleaning it will need."

Satisfied that she'd taken his advice, he shoved the keys into his pocket, and joined her on the sidewalk. Together, they walked into the shop where Damien had held his first job in high school. It had been a taste of financial freedom and a chance to get away from the house and his father. John and his friends sat there as they had a thousand times before, talking town gossip and politics over cans of Coke. They all looked up when the door chimed.

"My God. Look what the tide has washed in," John yelled over Axl Rose's voice belting "Sweet Child O' Mine" from the shop stereo. Gasoline, rubber, and sweat lingered in the air.

"Damien Trent and Lindsey Hunter—and a little musk-rat."

Lindsey clutched the dog in her arms. Damien recognized the fire chief, the one who'd served the town for nearly thirty years.

"I'm sorry about your father, son." He stood, clapped Damien on the shoulder. Lindsey's eyes met his, filled with apology.

"Nice to see you kids end up together, and with a baby on the way," John said.

Lindsey blushed, a deep pink rising on her cheeks. "Damien actually just stopped on the roadway to help...my car broke down."

He reached out and lightly touched her shoulder. It must suck, having to face all the unknowns of having a baby on her own. It took guts to return to this small town where gossip churned like a white-water rapid. People would speculate and judge.

They told John the location of the vehicle, and he promised to text Lindsey when it was finished. After they left the shop and were a few feet down the road, Lindsey grasped his arm to stop him.

"Damien, I'm so sorry about your father." She gently stroked his forearm. The tension in his muscles went lax under her fingertips.

He shrugged and started walking again. He didn't want to see the pity that swam in her eyes.

"I know your childhood wasn't easy, but all the same, you came here to grieve. The last thing you probably needed was to find me on the side of the road. I appreciate the lift, and your help."

"Took my mind off things." He slowed his pace to a crawl, realizing she was carrying a basketball-sized human in her belly and the dog, while he was plowing forward at a brisk clip. "Let me take her." He shifted Daisy out of her hands without waiting for a reply.

They reached the Seahorse Inn and every parking spot in front of the hotel was taken. Shit. He should have made reservations. In the chaos of it all, he'd forgotten how packed the hotels and motels got during the summer. He held the door for Lindsey and walked up to the front desk.

"Any vacancy?" he asked the woman behind the counter. Damien knew the answer before she opened her mouth. In the lobby, kids ran around in water shoes with soggy towels draping from their sunburnt shoulders. Their parents tried to corral them into the elevator with arms burdened with leftover picnic supplies and water boards.

"I'm sorry...we're sold out through the week. I'm afraid you won't have much luck at the other hotels, either. There's a convention in town. I could call around for you—save you a trip." Her concern seemed genuine and she began typing something into her desktop.

"I'd appreciate that. Thanks." Where were they going to stay if everything was sold out? He rolled his shoulders trying to ease the knot that rested between them.

Stress coiled in Damien's gut. He couldn't stay in his father's place. He'd have to drive a few hours inland, come back in the morning. Damien and Lindsey stood in silence, watching the unruly kids begin a sword fight with their pool noodles. Their parents' demands and threats fell on deaf ears. The dog tilted its head with each loud noise, but didn't bark.

He looked over at Lindsey. Her eyebrows were drawn together, and she bit her full bottom lip. "You ready for that?" Damien smiled at her, and tried to lighten the mood.

"God, I hope so." She let out a shaky laugh and wrapped her arms over her chest. "Listen, if there's no vacancy here you can crash with me for the night at the cottage. It's really no big deal."

He searched her face. There was no hesitation in her voice, no reservations, only a kind offer to an old friend. Under normal circumstances he'd brush it off, but he had so much to do. The wake was two days from now, the funeral after that, and then he was burdened with the task of cleaning out the house and listing it for sale.

His temples throbbed, like a marching band stomping and parading through his brain. The front desk agent beckoned to him, her face grim. Damien walked over to hear the news he could already read on her face.

"I'm sorry sir, no vacancy in Chatham tonight." The woman's voice was apologetic.

"Well, that settles it. Come on, bunkmate." Lindsey's fingers brushed his arm and a bolt of attraction zinged through him.

Lindsey was off-limits. Way off-limits. She was weeks away from delivering a baby—one that would need around-the-clock care, unlimited diaper changes, and would delight in lots and lots of squawking. He had enough baggage to fill a double-deck jet. Together, they would bring an airbus screeching to a halt. He'd spend the night, and figure things out in the morning with a clear mind and strong cup of black coffee.

Chapter Two

L INDSEY LOOKED PAST the dunes and swaying sea grass toward the rolling ocean. She ran a hand over her belly, the tumbling kicks of her active baby bumping against her hand. The intense movements reminded her that the baby was healthy and strong, and that she must be, too. It wasn't the way she'd planned on bringing her child into the world—a single parent with finances stretched to the brink of breaking. The day before hadn't been kind to her draining funds. She was sure car repairs would cost a pretty penny. Daisy circled in front of her feet and danced at the door, eager to be let outside.

Lindsey tiptoed quietly onto the porch, heard the sagging wood creak, and watched the dog race toward a sandpiper waddling across the beach. She shushed the dog's barks— Damien was still sleeping in the spare room. The fresh salt water air greeted her, the cry of gulls swooping over the shore line welcomed her. She'd come home to heal, to settle where her roots ran strong after her husband had made a fool of her. She'd been so naive during their short marriage.

Lindsey had used the money she'd squirreled away from

her position as an accountant to put a down payment on the cottage, before Matthew told her she needed to stay home and tend to her pregnancy. He hadn't really cared about her well-being, but it was more convenient to sneak around with his assistant while Lindsey was safely tucked away at home. She shook her head. When had she lost her spine?

The sliding door opened and Damien came out onto the porch, a five o'clock shadow peppering his face. The close-shaven military cut was a stark contrast to dark hair that swung to his collar in high school. There was a pull in her belly, one that had nothing to do with the baby's constant gymnastic performance. It had been hard to sleep with him right across the hall.

"That's a hell of a view you have," he said, as he looked toward the ocean.

"It makes the warped floors and peeling paint worth it." She laughed it off, though the worry ran bone-deep. In its current state, the cottage was no place to raise a child. It wasn't the well-kept waterfront home she remembered, but she'd have to make do with what she had. It was too late to back out now.

"Did it look like this when you toured it before purchase? The sellers are obligated to keep it in decent shape—you can go after them for the repairs, Lindsey." He stood firmly, looking ready to defend her. He looked better than the double chocolate brownies she'd been craving; his shirt was pulled taunt over his broad chest and tattoos he didn't have when he left the town snaked over his upper arm and added to the tough aura he carried. He caught her staring and she quickly looked out at the water.

Heat rushed to her cheeks. She'd purchased it sight-unseen, lured by distant memories and a chance to get far, far away from her husband and his infidelities. The price had been reasonable, and now she understood why.

"I can't." She caught a strand of hair the wind carried away and tucked it behind her ear. "I needed a place to stay, something permanent, and I purchased without seeing it first. The listing photos had looked decent…" Lindsey pushed her shoulders back when the urge to weep crashed over her like the waves slapping over the shore.

"You could stay at your folks' place while someone is re-habbing it," Damien suggested.

Lindsey laughed bitterly. Wasn't the reason she'd snapped it up to prove to her parents, to everyone, that she could stand on her own two feet and face life as a single parent without handouts and pitied glances?

"No." Her voice sounded stronger than it felt. "I'm going to stay. Once I pick up my car, I'm going to grab a mop at the store and start scrubbing. Things always look better clean."

Damien shot a doubtful look back at the cottage. "If you say so, Freckles."

She hadn't heard the silly nickname in a decade, and it still sent a warm flush through her. *What was wrong with her?*

She had been walked over, chewed up, spit out, and shot out of a cannon by her soon-to-be ex. Yet Damien still made her heart flutter and breath quicken after all this time.

As kids, she and Damien had been close. They skipped rocks at the pond behind her house, climbed trees, and finished their homework at the library after school. Damien had never wanted to go home. Then as eighth grade came to a close, they had an awkward encounter in a friend's closet during an unfortunate—or very fortunate depending on which side you were on—game of Spin the Bottle.

She'd never forget the moment when they had leaned in too quickly, bumped noses, and giggled nervously. They'd sure gotten it right the second try, though. He had touched her lips softly with his, pulled back to look at her, then drew her in again, deepening the kiss, running his hands over her hair. After that, Damien had distanced himself from her, and once they hit high school, he didn't even acknowledge her in the hallways.

"Let's hit the road. John said the car would be ready by nine o'clock, and he's never late." Damien pulled open the slider and stood back so she could go through first.

Her stomach knotted. The funds in her savings and checking account were dipping disastrously low. Everything was so tight. As long as the car didn't cost her an arm and a leg, she could make it work. She called Daisy who lifted her head from a hole she'd dug on the beach. A sandy mustache covered her snout.

"Hey, are you all right?" Damien touched her shoulder. "You look a little pale."

Lindsey mustered a smile. "I'm all right. Probably just a little flushed from the heat, or the watermelon-sized baby I'm carrying around." He returned her smile; it touched his impossibly blue eyes, and made her heart beat a little faster. Why did he have to look that good?

They got onto his bike and drove downtown to the shop. Just as she'd expected, the damn car ate a sizable chunk out of her checking account, but it couldn't be helped. After she bought a few groceries and cleaning supplies, she'd need to tighten her belt loop until she could find some type of employment.

Once outside the shop, Lindsey faced Damien on the sidewalk. The real reason Damien was back on the Cape was on her mind. It would be hard for him to lay to rest the man that caused him so much pain. Someone should be there to support him. "Thank you for your help. Really, I appreciate it. I'd like to attend your father's funeral, if it wouldn't be too obtrusive. I noticed the obituary said a private burial would be held."

He shoved his hands into his jean pockets. "It's not obtrusive. My father had a few aunts and uncles from Tennessee. It's going to be a small crowd. I'm going to the lawyer's office for the will reading this afternoon, and then the burial is tomorrow."

"And after that?" Lindsey shifted uncomfortably as the

baby pressed and prodded.

"Clean out the house, list it, and pray to God someone buys it." He surveyed the busy road. Cars chugged along Main Street; tourists on their way to play mini golf or shop for nautical treasures in a downtown store, like the one she'd dreamed of owning as a kid.

"Where will you stay in town?" Chatham was officially packed. The summer months always were. What would he do if he couldn't find a place to stay?

"I'll check the motels. There has to be vacancy somewhere."

"And if there's not?" Why did she kept pressing? Perhaps she was remembering the little boy who counted on her to stash a few snacks in her knapsack. She couldn't deny that having him in the next room the night before had taken away some of the loneliness.

"Worried about me, Freckles?" He grinned and the busy street faded away, the beeping cars, the thick throngs of tourists disappeared. All she could see was him; clear blue eyes and hard bronzed skin, dark closely shaven hair and an easy stance. Heat rushed to her cheeks, and suddenly the world tilted and swayed. Damien gripped her arms and steadied her.

"Whoa, take it easy now." Concern clouded his eyes and he kept his arms firmly around her. It was nice to be held, even just for a moment, in strong and secure arms.

"All of a sudden, everything was spinning. I'm okay now.

I shouldn't have skipped breakfast." She was in the third trimester and nausea still reared its ugly head in the morning, but the dizzy spell was a first.

"We'll fix that. Let's get you out of this heat." He grasped her hand. His palms were tough and callused. The contact sent a warm pang through her. Lindsey protested as he pulled her toward the diner.

"I can get something at home. It's not far from here." She couldn't keep dropping money on restaurant food.

"Consider it my payment for the lodging. Don't fight me, I'll win," he said. When he opened the door to the diner, an instantly refreshing burst of cold air hit her.

"What makes you so sure?" She smiled back at him now.

"Three tours in Iraq. Marine sniper." He grinned, arms crossed over his chest, and hip cocked to one side. Lindsey swallowed.

"I threw a punch at Marcy Robins in high school, but I think you have me beat." She put a hand against her back to ease the perpetual ache.

"I remember that. She was bullying a freshman and you came to the rescue." Damien's eyes twinkled. She swore she saw a flash of pride in them.

"And I was grounded for a month when the school called home." Her parents had flipped and she'd been stripped of her adolescent rights to talk on the phone and go to the mall. In the eyes of a teen, her world came to a halt. If only things were so simple now.

A waitress greeted them, and led them through the cramped dining room to a corner booth. Lindsey inhaled the smell of newly roasted coffee and looked longingly at the pot.

"Water is fine for me, thanks," she said when the waitress offered her a cup.

"I've been fantasizing about my post-pregnancy meal for months, and it includes coffee and red wine." Lindsey took a sip of water and wished it was something else.

"That's two liquids." He grinned at her, and her heart fluttered like a dragonfly was loose in her chest.

"Oh, the list goes on but I'm not sure you have time to hear it." They smiled at each other. Was that a hint of flirt that sparkled in his eyes? The waitress set down their drinks, then hurried to seat a new customer.

"I have a proposition for you." Damien took a gulp of black coffee and eyed her squarely.

She raised an eyebrow. "What's that?" Lindsey lowered her menu to face him fully.

"If I can't find a place in town, maybe you'll consider taking on a boarder. I'm guessing I'll be here for a little over a month to get my dad's place in better shape before I list it. I'd pay you the going rate for a motel in town." She hesitated, and he added, "It would be a win-win for both of us. I'd get a place to stay with a million-dollar view, and you'd get some extra cash for when the baby arrives."

The waitress came back, and they ordered. He'd struck a chord. She really needed additional money to prepare for the baby. Matthew had left her high and dry, taking her name off the joint accounts. It would hurt her pride to accept money from Damien, but logically his suggestion did make sense.

"Okay. You have a deal." He held out a hand and they shook on it. "Your stay at Casa de Lindsey will include breakfast, just like the area hotels, but no maid service." She smirked at him as the waitress set down their heaping plates. Her belly growled.

"Don't worry, I'm a big boy. I can pick up after myself." Damien spread a paper napkin on his lap, picked up a fork and dug into his scrambled eggs.

"That's good, because my current shape doesn't lend itself to scuba diving under the bed searching for dirty socks to wash."

He leaned back, looked her over. "Your shape is just fine, Lindsey."

Heat rushed to her cheeks. She might have believed he was sincere, if she didn't feel like a balloon, one that kept being pumped with helium to the point of bursting. The pregnancy glow had certainly passed her by, but not the morning sickness, the swollen ankles, or random bursts of acne she hadn't experienced even as a teenager. Lindsey hoped that after a rough pregnancy, nature would cut her some slack and give her a complication-free birth. At least her mother would be by her side, and her father in the waiting room. The thought of delivering the baby on her own, without a hand to hold or someone to lean on for support, scared her silly.

Damien crunched down a strip of bacon. Everything about him was rugged and strong, and just looking at him made her heart beat faster. It could be dangerous having him in the next room night after night, and nothing about her current situation was conducive to the steamy thoughts she was entertaining. She needed to focus on two things: providing for her baby and caring for him or her as a single parent. Lindsey couldn't let resurfacing feelings for Damien muddle her mind. She was not interested in romance, not after all she'd been through. It had to be all the hormones running through her body making her crazy, putting all these images in her mind. Was she strong enough to avoid the temptation? She hoped so, because like the purchase of the cottage, it was too late to turn back now.

Chapter Three

RAIN DRIZZLED FROM an ominous gray sky, and a handful of black umbrellas dotted the grave site. Damien stood with his jaw tight and lips stiff as the casket was lowered into the ground. Cold droplets trickled down his face to the edge of his tight collared shirt, like the tears he'd never be able to cry. He was being watched, and he knew instantly it was her. Lindsey had told him she would come, and she had. That held weight with Damien. So many people made promises, talked about things they'd do or wouldn't do, but at the end of the day, their actions didn't live up to the talk.

He glimpsed at her out of the corner of his eye, and caught a flash of the blond hair that trailed over her shoulders and flowed nearly to her waist. She wore a navy-blue dress that hugged her body and her rounded belly. Attraction coiled in his stomach. He still wanted her. He had always wanted her, but girls like Lindsey didn't belong with men like him. She would want a family man, someone who came home after their nine-to-five, and ate pot roast at the table before bouncing the baby on his knee. After his screwed-up childhood, he thought it best not to go down that route with anyone. He did best on his own and had excelled as a Marine, but now he didn't even have that. He had no idea what he was going to do next.

When the burial was over, he said a few words to his father's relatives, ones he hadn't seen in over twenty years. Lindsey stood near a cluster of trees waiting. Her hair whipped wildly as the storm intensified. He walked past columns of headstones to meet her.

"Thanks for coming." The drizzle changed to a downpour and thick droplets of cold rain pelted down on them.

"Get under my umbrella." Lindsey gently grasped his arm and pulled him close to her. He was already wet from standing without one during the burial, but there were worse things than being huddled next to Lindsey as the storm swirled around them.

"How are you holding up?" Her voice was gentle and sweet. He could listen to a voice like that all day.

"I'm fine. Part of me wishes I could feel sorry or sad. I just feel numb." *Why the hell had he shared that with her?* In her eyes he found kindness, and a judgement-free understanding. That was why. She hadn't changed a bit. Lindsey had been the only person he trusted enough to tell his secrets to. They often had talked about their dreams and fears as they watched fireflies glow over the dune grass. That had been before he kissed her, before the ground had shaken under his feet with the simple brush of lips. He'd had to distance himself from her then, because Lindsey had deserved better than the likes of him.

"You closed this chapter of your life when you left Chatham. You've already mourned for the father he never really was." She ran her hand down the sleeve of his shirt, and he fought the urge to pull her against him, and find comfort in her embrace. Instead, he stepped back, breaking the contact.

"Let's get out of here before we're both soaked through." Was that disappointment that swam in her eyes, or was it just him wishing it was there?

"Come in the car with me, Damien. You'll drown if you take your bike."

He shook his head. "I'll get your interior wet." He turned to walk toward the Harley. "See you at the cottage," he yelled over the rain pounding on the pavement.

"I don't care about the seat. It's just water. It'll dry." Her eyes pleaded with him. Damien didn't want to be in an enclosed space with her. He was already pinned under her spell.

"I'll see you at the cottage," he said again, needing to get away from her before he did something stupid. Damien swung a leg over the bike, kicked out the stand and revved the engine. The bike roared to life under him. It would be hard spending the next few weeks in the small seaside bungalow with Lindsey only a few feet away at any given moment.

He'd seen her carefully count her cash at the sandwich

shop, and then her shoulders slump slightly when the bill was presented at the garage. She was too proud to take a handout, so he had suggested they bunk together, even though the Seahorse Inn had phoned him to let him know of an unexpected vacancy. This was his chance to help her as she had helped him. He wouldn't screw it up by packing on more uncomfortable feelings for her.

As he pulled up to the cottage, he looked over the sandy hills teeming with tall grass, out to the choppy ocean waves. With a little work, this cottage would be a picturesque retreat. When he opened the front door, the little dog greeted him, its stump of a tail ticking back and forth. Daisy rolled over to expose her stomach, and her jowls fell back into a smile as he rubbed her belly. He'd dripped water all over the floor, and stood to get a towel.

"Leave it," Lindsey said as she entered the room. "There are clean towels for you in the bathroom. Toss your clothes outside the door and I'll throw them in the dryer."

Damien followed her directions; he knew not to mess with a pregnant lady. Besides, her voice held the quiet strength of his first drill sergeant. He went into the bathroom and cranked the water to steaming hot. The funeral had been the easy part; it was what came next that had his shoulders tight and his stomach in waves, just like the turbulent ocean outside. He hoped he could do what he needed to at the house without dredging up too many memories. The scorching water beat down on his skin for a good ten minutes before he shut it off and stepped out. Lindsey had left a few bath towels at the edge of the sink. He wrapped one around his waist, stepped out into the hallway, and square into Lindsey.

WARMTH RUSHED TO Lindsey's cheeks as she stood in the hallway, face-to-face with Damien. He'd come out of the bathroom and nearly knocked her over. Now he gripped her arms to keep her from toppling backward and strength rippled through his well-trained arms. His fresh-from-the-shower scent intoxicated her. She swallowed hard and couldn't keep her eyes from drifting down his torso, slick from the shower, to where a towel was tied loosely around his narrow hips. A jagged and deep scar snaked over his side, reminding her that he had seen the horrors of war. When she looked up, he was staring down at her. The heat from Damien's bare skin pulsed into her fingertips. Her heart beat quickly as his eyes dropped to her lips. What was happening? The Damien she had known in high school had avoided her like a case of the chicken pox after their first kiss. Why would he want to repeat it? He'd made it quite clear after their Spin the Bottle encounter that he wanted nothing to do with her—and yet his pupils widened, spilling inky black over the light blue of his irises until his eyes were dark and intense. Damien leaned closer until they were only inches apart. He tightened his grip on her elbows and drew her against him, brushing his lips over hers.

If their first kiss had been fireworks, this was a nuclear explosion. A bolt of heat shot through her and she tangled her arms around his shoulders. His tongue played over hers and need spun through her. When he backed her against the wall and deepened the kiss, she couldn't stop a sigh from escaping her throat.

To her disappointment, he abruptly broke off the kiss and looked down at her. Surprise widened his eyes. "I think your baby just gave me a warning kick." His voice was low and breathless. "She wants hands off her mama."

Lindsey let out a shaky laugh. She wasn't quite steady after that kiss. Hell, she hadn't been steady since she'd bumped into him on the side of the road. "What makes you so sure it's a girl?"

"I just have a feeling." He brushed a thumb over her cheek. "Sweet, pretty, like you."

"Damien." She pulled him closer, not ready for the moment to end. The towel did a poor job of concealing his physical reaction to her. Warmth enveloped her like someone had taken a thick towel straight from the dryer and pulled it tight around her body. Tingles coursed over her skin, like a thousand butterfly wings sashaying up her spine. It could have been the baby weight, but suddenly her knees didn't feel up to the task of holding her. She'd never been so undone, except once. That one night in the closet with

Damien.

"Lindsey, everything about this is a mistake." His voice was gruff and sexy. She wanted nothing more than to pick up where they left off, but she could already feel him closing a wall around himself. Damien ran a hand over her hair before he turned, walked down the hall to his room, and shut the door behind him. The scar that wound down his side was nothing compared to the mutilation that zigzagged sharply down his back.

Was that part of the reason he'd left the military? He hadn't said it, but she was sure he wouldn't have received so much time off for a bereavement leave, and he said he planned to stay for a month or so. His loose timeline told her he'd cut off his career with the Marines, or something had prevented him from returning.

Lindsey went into the kitchen and took out a frying pan from under the stove. The dog sat behind her like a shadow, anticipating her every move as she made her favorite comfort food. She put a pat of butter in the sizzling pan and dropped in two slices of bread. She couldn't think past the taste of Damien's lips or how his hard body had pressed up against her. She put cheese on the bread, added slices of ripened tomato, and stacked the two pieces together. While it melted together inside the pan, she turned and indulged Daisy with a piece of American cheese before sliding the sandwich onto a plate. She repeated the process, and replayed the kiss in her mind, going over every detail until she was thoroughly worked up.

He had said it was a mistake, and the hurt of rejection had launched pain into her heart and tightened her throat. She hadn't been able to keep the eye of her husband, what made her think she could keep the eye of Damien? She shook her head. If she was to be a strong single parent, she'd have to develop more of a backbone. Damien didn't want to be involved with her. Well, that was just fine. She had an overflowing bucket of worry as it was, without adding a man to the mix. She set both plates on the table, and knocked on Damien's door to let him know she'd made lunch. He wouldn't catch her off guard next time. From now on, this would be a business relationship only. Her heart and her mind couldn't deal with anything else.

Chapter Four

DAMIEN INHALED THE salty air and let it fill his lungs. The remote beach stretched on for miles without another person in sight, only shells and sand, seaweed and the occasional piece of driftwood. A reddish-gold glow painted the horizon, reminding him of the old mariners' rhyme, "Red sky at night, sailors' delight. Red sky at morning, sailors take warning." He should have taken a warning before kissing Lindsey. As the kiss had changed from tender and sweet to an intensity that had nearly knocked him off his feet, he'd wanted nothing more than to drag her into bed. Then the baby had given him a swift kick and reminded him that Lindsey was off-limits and he'd screwed up again.

When he pulled away he'd seen her flushed cheeks, the way her lips were swollen from rubbing against his. Desire clouded her wide eyes, and he'd almost drawn her back against him. He crouched down, picked up a flat rock, and flung it into the ocean. It hopped over the surf until it disappeared beneath the waves. What was he doing anyway? Lindsey was tremendously pregnant and looked as if she were ready to have her baby any day now. Whenever he got close, her belly bump pressed into him. It should have turned him off completely. Not because she wasn't beautiful—she was as gorgeous as ever—but she had just as much, if not more, baggage than him. And once the baby came…

Kids had always made him uneasy. He wasn't sure how to interact with them and he wasn't sure he'd be the best role model for one. A child deserved someone they could look up to. Someone they could trust. And why was he even thinking about how he'd interact with Lindsey's kid? Clearly her impending motherhood did nothing to curb his desire for her, or stop him from playing out scenarios in his head. Ones where he could be the type of man she deserved. But what did it matter? He was only here temporarily. He could help her in the short-term, but permanence wasn't an option for him.

Thoroughly annoyed with himself, he picked up another rock and chucked it into the blue. As it skipped out toward the horizon line, another rock hopped past it, traveling feet beyond its own. His adrenaline surged, and he spun to his right. His tightened shoulders eased when he saw Lindsey standing there with a smug look on her face.

The sound of rushing waves had masked her approach and caught him off guard. He'd been ambushed during a mission in Afghanistan and it had cost him his best friend, and a good soldier. It had been his fault. Johnny's blood would always stain his hands. Breathe in, breathe out. He did that, until the knot in his stomach eased and images of blood pumping over the sunbaked sand subsided. The dog yipped, bringing him back to the present. Daisy dug through washed-up seaweed at Lindsey's feet; the dog rarely left her side.

"I'm still better than you." Lindsey smirked and held up another rock. "Best out of three?"

"Loser makes breakfast." His lips instantly curved and he bent to find a stone.

She did the same, crouching awkwardly in the sand to look for a rock.

"Not sure I'm in the mood for scorched eggs," she said. When Lindsey's face lit with a playful grin, his nerve endings awakened and stirred. A seagull cried out in the distance, waves ebbed and flowed with a rhythmic whoosh-whoosh. The sounds of the beach made a serene orchestra around them.

"Good, because we'll be having omelets whipped up by Executive Chef Hunter." He wiped crumbly damp sand off a decent-sized rock, tossed it in the air, and caught it. "Get your spatula ready, Freckles," Damien said. Something jerked inside him when her playful laugh filled the air.

He pulled his arm back, snapped his wrist forward, and propelled his rock past Lindsey's. Damien let out a victory whoop. "I can practically smell those omelets now," he said.

A determined look stole over her features, and on the final round, her rock sailed by his, putting his throw to shame.

"I bet you look good in an apron, Damien. I'm going to enjoy the view over my burnt toast." Lindsey stood with a hand on one hip and the other absently rubbing her swollen belly.

They both chuckled when Daisy popped up from the sand, a seaweed halo shrouding her head. The dog danced wildly trying to get it off, before Damien plucked it off her head. He had a soft spot for dogs. When he was a kid cowering in his bedroom, as the downstairs TV blared, and the smell of stale booze pumped through the air, he would imagine having a dog. One that would snarl when his drunk father had the urge to punch something. They went inside the cottage, and Lindsey scooped up Daisy.

"I'm going to wash some of this seaweed off Daisy. Feel free to look through the boxes. There are more cooking supplies somewhere." He watched her leave the room, and appreciated the way her yoga pants clung to her body. *Cool it.* He was no better than a hormonally-charged teen.

Damien started rummaging through boxes. He opened one that was filled with oil paints. Lindsey had always been a talented artist, and he was glad she hadn't given it up. He found some supplies, put a pan on the stove, and turned up the heat.

Despite his best efforts, the eggs were singed around the sides and the toast was dark. When he tested it though, it wasn't that bad. Probably the pound of butter he'd slathered over the toast, and the cheese he'd sprinkled liberally on the eggs to mask the burn.

"I take back all my comments. This isn't half-bad, Damien." A smile bloomed over her cheeks, and he looked down at his eggs. Maybe he'd find a remedy for the crazy feelings she ignited within him somewhere in the scrambled mass.

"Don't get used to it. I almost singed off a finger." He bit into the toast, eyeing her over the crusty bread.

"You have ten of them." She gave him a sassy smirk, cupped her mug of warmed water and lemon, and lifted it to her plump lips. His pulse kicked up. Those lips had been against his, so pliant and full of need.

"I don't remember you being so cheeky," Damien said.

Lindsey's gaze dropped to her hands. "A lot's changed." She laced her fingers together. "Spending time with you reminds me of how I used to be."

"What do you mean?" His stomach shifted uncomfortably.

"I used to be so independent, and now..." The dog whined and circled at her feet. "My ex used to come up with the most logical reasons for why I should do things a certain way, dress in particular clothes, let him control the finances because it was easier to keep everything under his name. I just went along with it."

Damien's jaw tightened and he wanted to plant a fist in the son of a bitch ex-husband's face. Instead he reached across the table and gripped her hand.

"The woman sitting in front of me is as self-sufficient as it gets. You left him—that takes courage." He squeezed her hand to reinforce his words.

"I couldn't stay." Lindsey's cheeks reddened. "Not after I walked in on him and his assistant. I had baked brownies and thought it would be nice to bring him a plate. When I opened his office door, his pants were around his ankles, and a naked woman was sprawled on his desk." Her shoulders slumped; an invisible weight seemed to press against them.

"Lindsey, look at me." He locked his eyes on hers. "Whatever he did is no reflection on you. It doesn't make you weak. It doesn't make you stupid. It just makes him a horrible fucking husband, and a sorry excuse for a man." Damien rubbed his thumb over her knuckles. He was about to go to her, when her phone's ringtone sliced through the air.

He released her hand and she glanced at the number on the screen.

"Excuse me," she said, and walked across the room to take the call. He got up, cleared their plates, and busied himself with the dishes. Whoever was on the other line was seriously stressing her out. She paced near the glass doors and pinched the bridge of her nose.

"Everything okay?" He finished drying the last plate and turned to look at Lindsey. She dropped the phone to her side.

"It was my parents. They're coming home early." Lindsey crossed her arms over her chest and looked out at the beach.

"Is that a bad thing?" To his memory Lindsey had always been close to her parents.

She sighed and turned her attention back to Damien. "I don't want them to see what a disaster this cottage is. The place I've chosen to bring their grandchild into the world. I need more time…"

Damien's chest clenched. He could read between the lines—she didn't have the money, or the time to fix this place. She sure as hell couldn't do it on her own in her current state. Now her parents were coming back unexpectedly and she didn't even have a nursery set up for the baby.

Damien jammed his hands into his jean pockets. "I wish I could help you, but organizing my father's belongings and listing the house is going to eat up all my time. I'd much rather be doing physical labor than sorting through boxes of worthless junk. As it is, I hired a cleaning service for Wednesday. I have to have all the crap out by then, so the Realtor can take pictures. I haven't even pulled in the driveway yet." His muscles tensed like taunt elastic bands every time he thought of going back to the house, the one he swore he'd never step foot in again. It needed to get done, so he could put Chatham behind him for good.

His actions had already been derailed. When he came back to town, he asserted that he wouldn't let anything distract him. Get in, get out. That was the plan. A block of ice pressed in his gut when he pictured going back in that house and going through his father's paperwork and knick-knacks. Working with his hands would be a welcome relief.

"I'm kind of a whiz at organizing." Lindsey looked at him inquisitively, and turned her head to the side. He could practically see a light bulb go off over her head. "We could do a house swap. I can't do much physical work, but I can help you go through papers, and maybe list some stuff on eBay?"

Damien considered it. While it wouldn't get him out of going to the house altogether, it certainly would take away the pains and frustrations of going through boxes. He could rent a U-Haul, load up the junk, and never step over the threshold again. If Lindsey could sort through the stuff at the cottage, it would give the Realtor plenty of wiggle room to take pictures, install the lock box, and schedule showings.

"A house swap, huh? You might regret that offer." Damien searched her face looking for any sign that she might want to rescind her suggestion.

"I don't think so. I'd be getting a lot more out of the deal than you would be," she said.

Damien looked around the cottage. It needed new paint, replaced flooring, some sturdier planks on the deck but all in all, the work was mostly cosmetic. It would be a cinch to have the cottage parent-ready in a few weeks if he could give it his undivided attention. He had to admit, he wouldn't mind spending more time at the cottage. Being with Lindsey made him forget the sound of shells exploding around his feet, and Johnny's lopsided grin. She made him forget all the reasons he hated Chatham—the hunger that had constantly coiled in his belly, the fear that gripped him every day after school, the trouble that had constantly plagued him as a teen.

"I can pack things into boxes and bring them here to sort through. We can keep them in the garage, and bring them in one at a time. You'll need to pick paint colors for the house, because it could sure use a fresh coat inside and out."

"I'll go with you to the house and help pack things up." She held up a hand to stop his protest. "It's only fair. You can do all the heavy lifting but I can at least put things into boxes and wrap up the valuables. It will go faster with two."

She was right. And having her there meant he wouldn't have to wallow in his own thoughts. "Okay. How does tomorrow sound?" he said.

"As good as any, partner." She held out a hand to shake on it. Her palm was soft as silk and her hand wrapped neatly inside his.

Their wager would offer a fresh start for both of them; Damien could list the house in less time, and Lindsey would have something of her own that she could be proud of. He would have to be sure to keep his distance from her as he worked at the cottage. If he wasn't careful, he could get wrapped up in a girl like Lindsey, and he already had a lot of untangling to do in his own life. Besides, he wasn't planning on staying in Chatham. Damien wasn't sure what he'd do after their pact was complete, but staying in this small seaside town had never been part of his future agenda. Not now. Not ever.

Chapter Five

As LINDSEY AND Damien drove toward the outskirts of Chatham, the number of homes and businesses thinned, the trees edging the road became thicker, and Damien became quieter. The only sound in the rented U-Haul cab was the static buzz from the radio that couldn't find a station. She viewed his profile. He sat straight as an arrow, every inch of hard muscle was taut with stress. His jaw was clenched so hard, his teeth probably ached.

She'd had her doubts about the wager she'd made with him the night before, as she lay in bed with a kickboxing session going on inside her stomach. A million doubts and fears had raced through her mind. She was so close to her due date. What if she couldn't uphold her end of the bargain? What would her parents think when they found out she'd been sharing a house with a man, when the ink was barely dry on her divorce papers? Most of all, she wondered how she'd survive the typhoon of emotions that crashed over her every time she got close to Damien. Whenever he came near, her pulse hammered and she was immersed in a flood of desire. And man, on a rare occasion when a smile stretched over his lips, the world seemed to wash away around her.

She had to avoid temptation. The baby was number one—always. She bit her lip, and a trickle of guilt filtered through her. Lindsey had been thinking of Damien almost as much as her impending due date—what kind of mother did that make her? No, losing her focus over a handsome face and rugged body just wouldn't do. She'd do her best to make it a friendly business transaction between friends, nothing more. They'd get in the house, pack up the stuff, and go home. No harm, no foul.

But when they pulled up to the weathered gray shingled house, and his hands gripped the wheel like a life preserver, Lindsey ached to reach out to him.

"We're here." His voice was low and gritty. For a moment, he just stared. The steep roof had two dormered windows on either side of a central chimney. She wondered if Damien had looked out of one of those windows as a child, longing for his mother. Lindsey gave him a moment, and then rallied for them both.

"Let's get in, pack up, and get out. Okay?" She gave him what she hoped was a look of encouragement, and was relieved when he nodded and opened the driver's side door. Damien carried a stack of flat boxes while she took packing tape, scissors, and permanent markers for labeling. He slid the key into the lock, jimmied it around, and pushed open the door. The inside smelled dank and stale—a yeasty,

skunky scent left behind by the empty beer cans that crowded the end table beside a slumped couch. Damien stood,
hands against his sides, taking it in.

"You hired a cleaning crew, so we just need to take out
the belongings." She had to keep him focused and distracted.

"I don't even know where to begin." He ran a hand over
his cropped black hair.

"Let's try room by room. Should we start upstairs or
down?" she asked.

"Upstairs first." He looked at the stairwell but didn't
move, so she walked ahead of him.

Lindsey took the steps slowly and held on to the railing—it was hard to navigate stairs when she couldn't see
what was under her feet. There were two bedrooms on the
upper level, and she chose one at random. Damien needed
someone to take the lead. When he walked into the room,
she slipped a box from his hands, folded the bottom, and
secured it with tape. She repeated the process until they had
three boxes ready to be packed.

Damien cleared his throat. "This was my father's room.
We can donate all the clothes."

"Okay, then." Lindsey took a box to the closet. Before
she opened it, she turned to face him. "Damien, is there
anything I should keep?"

He shook his head. "Nothing." He snapped open one of
the cedar drawers. She followed his lead, taking piles of
clothes and stuffing the boxes. They moved at a quick clip

and were done packing the room much faster than she'd expected. They moved on to the next. This room had baseball posters and a bright blue bedspread. Little League awards scattered the shelf that hung over the headboard. A small desk sat in the corner along with a beanbag chair. Damien's room. She glanced over at him and her heart burned.

Lindsey could see the memories play over his face. It must be hard, to have no good ones to comfort. Despite her earlier pep talk to keep her hands off, she closed the distance between them, and wrapped her arms around his neck. She had meant for it to be a quick hug, but his arms circled around her and kept her firmly in place. He rested his chin lightly on the top of her head, and she leaned into his hard chest. His heart drummed a steady beat against her cheek. Something in her heart tugged and pulled, when he tightened his embrace and kissed the top of her head. Had she ever wanted someone so much? When the baby pelted her, sending a bolt of pain ricocheting through her rib cage, she pulled back and grimaced.

Damien grabbed her shoulder. "Are you okay?" His eyes were intense as he scanned her face.

She took a deep breath, as the discomfort faded. "I might be growing a sumo wrestler, or a future WWE wrestler in there." It was good to hear him chuckle, and some of the tension that hung thickly in the air dissipated.

He held his hand just above her belly. "Can I?" he asked,

sounding not quite sure of himself.

She nodded, unable to form a coherent sentence. He laid his big palm across her stomach. Lindsey knew the moment he felt the baby wriggle. His face, which was hard from stress, softened. His hand traced the movement of the baby as it rolled and pressed against her side. He lifted his gaze and locked his eyes on hers. Her breath caught and her throat tightened. Something about this intimate moment seemed big and important. Unspoken needs and the movements of the baby hung in the space between them. He broke away abruptly, and her heart shrank.

"That was something else. I've never felt a baby kick before." His voice was unsteady and strained. He wasn't as immune to her as he pretended to be. She could hear the heavy longing in his tone. The space he'd created gave her time to regain her composure and she taped together two new boxes.

Needing some distance from him, she slid over one of the boxes. "If you don't mind, I'll do the hall closet, and then move downstairs."

"Okay," he said with his gaze still fastened on her. "Be careful on those stairs."

Once she was out of his sight, she released the breath she'd been holding. Damien's face had filled with awe when he had felt the baby move—the way a man should look when he feels his baby kick for the first time. Except Damien wasn't the father. The baby's real father wouldn't relinquish full parental rights to Lindsey, but still wanted to start "fresh" with his assistant. He'd made it clear that she and the baby weren't part of his future. At the moment, it seemed like her life was a jumbled mess and Damien wasn't making it easy to stay focused. She gave herself a few more moments, and then started on the closet.

WHEN DAMIEN JOINED Lindsey downstairs, he found her humming by the kitchen sink. She reached both arms up to the cabinet and arched her back slightly to pull down a copper pot. The tips of her hair tumbled to the small of her back. He'd like to run his fingers through it. He imagined that hair flowing over his pillow like morning sun streaming through the window. He'd move over her slowly and her creamy bare skin would be like silk against his. She'd sigh his name and tangle her arms around his neck. Damien shook his head. He had to get his shit together.

He jumped toward her when the stack of bowls above her teetered at the edge of the shelf. Damien shifted his arms above Lindsey's head to steady the dishes, pinning her gently against the laminate. He glanced down at her. Was it his imagination, or did a hunger steal over her features? The look disappeared as fast as it had come. There was no desire in her eyes now, and she angled her body, spun under his arms, and slipped the wooden cutting board she was holding into the box.

"That was a close one. I didn't realize packing was such perilous work." She flashed him a grin that made his body stir. They tackled the basement together next. He stood on a step ladder to reach things on the built-in shelving and passed them down to Lindsey where she wrapped and stowed them in boxes. There wasn't much to pack, but they made a good team all the same.

At noon, he went to get them subs. She insisted on staying to finish the hall closet. Damien called in the order before he started the rental truck—chicken salad for her, Italian for him—lunchtime was pure insanity during tourist season. As he navigated the familiar roads, he realized he'd barely succumbed to the hard memories of his childhood all day. Except for the initial sights and smells of the house after so many years, he'd really only thought of one thing while they were there—Lindsey. That was a problem he'd have to explore at a later time, but for now he was stronger with her by his side, helping to shoulder the work of packing away memories. No matter how bad, they were his. The final act of tucking things into boxes was like a final farewell to the boy he'd once been and the life he'd once lived.

When he returned to the house with lunch, she greeted him at the door.

"Boy am I glad to see you. Packing works up an appetite." She took the two bottles of water he was holding to the kitchen table.

"Sure does." He unwrapped one of the subs, saw it was his and gave her the other. "Didn't think I was going to make it out of town alive," he said between bites. "Tourists are animals around mealtime."

"Try a pregnant woman." She laughed. "I was ready to start chewing on the side of the table."

They ate quietly for a few minutes—an easy, comfortable quiet.

"How are you holding up?" she asked after a while.

"It's been easier having you here," he said over the top of his sub. "I guess I was a little surprised to see my bedroom still intact. When I decided to enlist, my father said if I left, there wouldn't be a place for me when I returned." What if the glassy look in his father's eyes when he left hadn't only been from the alcohol?

"His way of asking you to stay," she said hitting the nail on the head.

"It wasn't about wanting me here, though." Damien drained his water and crumpled the plastic bottle in his hand. "He didn't want me to leave like my mother did."

"Did he save any of her things?" Lindsey asked and rested a hand over her belly.

"The day she left, he started a bonfire in the backyard. He was drunk and wild with rage, and he started chucking her things into it left and right." He had cried, screamed, and pulled at his father's leg. He had tossed away what was left of his mother, when Damien had wanted to hold on like

48

his life depended on it.

His heart hardened against the memory. If he didn't think of it objectively, it would break him. "I was clinging onto one of her old shirts. It smelled like her, and I wanted to keep it. He ripped it from me and threw it into the fire." His jaw tightened. That was the moment he knew his life would never be the same.

"Oh, Damien. I'm so sorry. I can't even imagine the hurt…" Her eyes misted and she reached across the table for his hand.

"You love your baby already. It's all over your face when you feel it kick. I hear you singing lullabies at night, and it's in your voice. It makes me wonder how she walked away from her son. Her only child." He hadn't thought about being abandoned in so long, and was taken off guard at the intensity of the anger burning inside him.

"It wasn't you, Damien. You know that, right?" She searched his face and lifted a hand to his cheek. "There's no reason she could have possibly had, that would bring you comfort, but her own demons drove her to leave, not you."

"Her smile never really reached her eyes. Somedays she'd lock herself in her room and would cry in the dark for hours. Then she'd reappear the next day, over-the-top excited, talking a mile a minute, and spin me around until we both fell onto the floor dizzy and laughing." He pushed away from the table and started clearing the remnants of lunch. Lindsey's chair scraped against the floor, and she came over to him. For the second time that day, he accepted her embrace and let himself lean on someone else for just a little bit.

"You're going to be a terrific mother, Lindsey," he murmured into her hair. Her scent, something warm and cozy like vanilla and cinnamon, tickled his senses. "You already are."

"And someday, when the time's right, you'll be a wonderful father." When he scoffed, she added, "You're not like your parents, Damien. Don't let life pass you by because you're afraid of being wired like them." She locked eyes with him, and fierceness filled her face. "You're not." She pressed her lips quickly to his, and just as fast moved away.

They worked side by side for the rest of the afternoon, sealing items in bubble wrap, packing boxes, and chatting about lighter topics. Soon all the boxes were stacked in the U-Haul and there was only one place left to tackle. They walked outside to his father's work area. Damien had never been allowed into the shed that stood feet from the house. The red door was rotted and paint flaked off, revealing the plywood underneath. His heart beat faster when he stood face-to-face with the door, like his father might pop out and tan his hide for getting too close.

He turned the knob but the door wouldn't budge. Damien used his shoulder to force it open and fell through the threshold when it gave way.

"Careful," he warned Lindsey. "I've never been in here,

so I'm not sure if the floorboards are steady, or if there are any surprises." She heeded his advice and stepped in gingerly, testing the wood planks before choosing a spot to stand.

A weak stream of sunlight filtered through the dirty windows, offering just enough light to see the disarray of the room. The walls of the small space were lined with hanging tools, a fishing pole, and lures. The workspace was cluttered with more beer cans, an orange toolbox, and remnants of an unfinished project. Damien was surprised to see a safe on the bottom shelf of the workbench. He tried a few combinations, his birthdate, his father's birthdate, but the lock stayed securely clamped shut. His breath quickened when he thought of another date. His fingers carefully spun a new combination into the lock: the day his mother left. The lock clicked and released. Now that he could see what was inside, he didn't want to look. Whatever his father stowed away in a safe wasn't meant for his eyes. He looked back at Lindsey and she stood there patiently. She seemed to understand he wanted her presence, but let him have the moment in quiet.

Releasing a breath, he opened the safe. The plastic bag inside made his heart thump faster. Through the clear bag, he could see a swatch of pink that frayed into a burnt mess. The shirt Damien had wanted to keep when his mother left. He lifted it gingerly out, and for a moment just stared. His father must have pulled it out of the fire when Damien ran inside. Maybe part of him had cared after all.

A hard lump formed in Damien's throat. He reached

back into the safe and pulled out framed photographs that disappeared the day she left. He picked one up, in hands that shook, and the smiling faces of his mother, father, and baby Damien looked back. Lindsey had crept up behind him and gently kneaded his tight shoulders. He reached back into the dark safe and trailed his fingers around the edges. His hand brushed over a piece of paper and he grasped it. It was a crayon drawing of three stick figures, signed with a wobbly signature.

"I can't believe he kept this stuff. I thought he hated her for leaving and hated me more because somehow it was my fault," Damien said after a while. "He would tell me that from time to time—if I was better, smarter, she would have stayed."

"He was in pain," Lindsey said softly. "And lashed out at a small defenseless boy to ease the hurt."

"I've had enough for one day. Let's get out of here." He was grateful when she didn't pry, and on the ride home left him to his own thoughts. Occasionally, she reached over to brush a hand over his shoulder to comfort. She had an instinctive and intimate awareness of his moods. He was alarmed by how much he wanted her, but more so, he was terrified of the affection that spread through him every time she was near. They meshed so well together—always had. In the back of his mind though, he'd always see his father's face the day his mother backed out of the driveway and never returned. It had crushed him, broke him, and turned him into someone hard and cold. That look was the reason Damien had distanced himself from Lindsey after their first youthful kiss. One brush of lips in a dark closet made him aware that she had the power to irreversibly untwine him— body, mind, and soul.

Chapter Six

FOR THE NEXT few days, they kept their distance. Neither of them was ready to explore the emotional landslide that had happened at Damien's father's house. Lindsey busied herself sorting and organizing, and tried to ignore the uncomfortable stomachache that had plagued her off and on all morning. She chalked it up to stress and the eggs Damien had made for breakfast. Damien had held true to his end of the deal so far and scrapped, hammered, and measured. A few times she'd looked out the window and seen his bare chest and arms rippling in the hot sun as he worked. She'd closed the blinds after that. At some point, Daisy had hopped up on the couch beside her and nestled against her leg. The dog's soft snores mingled with the Top 40, as she opened envelope after envelope, decided if it was important, and either set it aside for Damien or fed it through the shredder.

Lindsey gasped and froze at the sudden pop inside her. Liquid rushed between her legs. "Oh, my God," she whispered. Damien had just walked into the kitchen and she called out to him.

"What's wrong?" He quickly strode toward her. When he saw the pool of water spreading over the floor, his brows shot up. "It's not time yet. Is it?" he questioned.

"I think the baby is ready to make an early appearance." She put a hand on her side when a dull pain squeezed around her belly. Damien dropped to the floor beside her and held her hand. "If that's how the first contraction feels, I'm not looking forward to the rest of them." She grimaced.

When the ache subsided, she released his hand.

"Do you have a bag for the hospital?" Damien eyes darted around the room.

"I didn't think I'd have a need of one yet." She sat helplessly as more water rushed onto the floor. "The stomachaches I've been feeling—it must have been the start of labor. I thought it was your cooking." She smiled a little.

"Gee, thanks." He squeezed her knee, then got up, and jumped into action. She watched as he gathered towels from the hall closet and spread them over the floor. Damien disappeared into his room and reappeared with an empty duffel bag.

"I'm going to pack some of your things, okay?" he asked.

She nodded and concentrated on the second wave of pain. Was it supposed to start this quickly? Feel this intense? She did her best to remain calm. Panicking wouldn't help her or the baby get through this. Damien came back and handed her a pair of yoga pants and a T-shirt.

"Do you need help changing?" He kneeled down and

switched the sopping towel on the floor with a dry one. Heat rose on her cheeks.

"No, I can handle it." She went into the bathroom and slowly pulled on the pants and T-shirt. Her toothbrush was gone from the holder by the sink, as was the toothpaste, and her hairbrush. Even though she was slightly bashful that he was witnessing her most vulnerable moments, Lindsey was thankful she wasn't alone. When she emerged, Damien was filling Daisy's bowl with dry food and getting her fresh water.

"I'm guessing we might be a while." He slung the over-stuffed duffel over his shoulder. What could he have possibly packed that had it stretching at the seams? He took her car keys off the counter, put his hand on the small of her back, and led her gently to the car. Damien spread a towel on the passenger seat, and moved aside so she could sit.

"Do you want me to readjust the seat? Would you be more comfortable leaning back?"

She shook her head and rubbed her belly as another wave hit—stronger this time. If the stomach pains she'd experienced earlier had been contractions, too, maybe she was farther along than she thought. She gripped the side of the seat, knuckles going white, as she considered the timing. She was only thirty-seven weeks. Lindsey knew from *What to Expect When You're Expecting* that the dangers of an early birth decreased each week. What if her baby needed more time, though? Would the baby be strong enough? Was it too soon?

Every so often, she could feel Damien's eyes on her. Each time they hit a red light, impatience simmered off him like the steam rising from a boiling pot.

By the time they pulled up to the hospital, sweat beaded over Lindsey's brow. When a contraction hit, a vise gripped her insides and twisted. The pain radiated around her belly and across her back. Damien passed the keys off to the valet attendant, took the duffel from the backseat, and rushed to the passenger door. He helped her stand, and together they walked into the hospital. Lindsey checked in as Damien stood closely behind her. They were directed straight to triage. Lindsey lay on the metal rollaway bed covered by a paper protector, and shortly after a nurse pulled open the blue-and-white curtain.

"Nice to meet you both." She smiled at Damien, then at Lindsey. "My name's Tina and I'm the RN here in triage." When she looked down at Lindsey's file, her cropped chestnut hair skimmed just above her jawline. Tina began asking Lindsey questions.

How far apart are the contractions? How many weeks are you?

"Okay, then," Tina said eventually. "Let's get this baby on the radar and see what it's up to."

She put a band around Lindsey's stomach and tucked in round monitors. Damien sat in a chair nearby and rubbed her shoulder steadily each time a contraction hit.

"The contractions are coming close. Let's see how far you're dilated," Tina said, and draped a sheet over Lindsey's legs. Lindsey was momentarily embarrassed having Damien there, but when the next contraction broke over her, strong and painful, she gripped his arm.

"Don't worry," he whispered in her ear. "I'm right here, and I'm not leaving."

"All right." Tina looked up with a delighted grin. She was so cheerful, Lindsey wanted to snap. "It's almost show-time. You're eight centimeters dilated—fast for a first-timer." She rolled the wheeled chair to the computer and punched in some data. "How are you handling the pain?" Tina asked.

"It's okay." Lindsey gritted her teeth. It hurt like hell.

"I'm not sure what you had planned for pain management, but at this point the baby will probably be out before we can get an epidural."

"I hadn't planned on one," Lindsey said through short pants. "But I sure wish I had."

She was wheeled down the white sterile hall to a birthing room. Damien was a constant source of comfort through the pain. He gave her an anchor when distress threatened to overcome her. The contractions became stronger and stronger, until she thought she couldn't bear another moment. Her body was exhausted from fielding the intensity of labor, and she hadn't even started pushing yet.

"You're doing amazing, Lindsey." Damien encouraged her and ran a hand over her hair. "Keep fighting."

When it was time, she bore down with all her might. The pain was an enormous force that overtook her body and mind. She was so tired, and the man that should have been by her side was uninterested in the birth of their baby. She was so confused by all the feelings she had for the man who stood beside her now. She was just divorced, yet she found herself slipping into love with Damien. He was so many things and the combination lured her. Hard yet kind. The type of kindness that moved him to not only rescue her from the side of the road, but stay with her at the shop. The type of kindness that packed a hospital bag and offered encouragements and endearments throughout the trials of labor. A warrior with deep scars and eyes that held painful secrets— the same eyes lit when her baby kicked against his hand.

Lindsey looked over at Damien, and was so thankful for him. He held on to her like a steady anchor in a swirling storm. In his eyes, she found the strength she needed to make the final push. The pain was so great, she cried out. Suddenly, it subsided and she heard a cry, then another. Lindsey sobbed in relief as the baby was placed on her chest.

"Congratulations," the doctor said. "It's a healthy baby girl."

So precious and small, this tiny life was the most miraculous thing that had ever happened to her. Lindsey imprinted the moment in her brain, the sound of her little girl's first cries, the way her tiny hands fisted tightly, the downy fuzz that wisped over her head, but most of all the magical emotions that wrapped around her heart. She sighed and nuzzled closer to the baby. Overcome and overwhelmed with the moment, she had forgotten Damien was still in the room. She glanced up at him, and the strangest look swam in his eyes. Was it pride she saw there? Relief?

"What will you call her?" He stepped closer to the bed, and ran his thumb over the baby's cheek. Her daughter's hand reached out and grasped his finger, like a seahorse curling around ocean grass. Her heart faltered at the sight of the baby's tiny pink finger wrapped around Damien's.

"Maris." She smiled. "It means *of the sea*."

"Maris." He spoke it slowly, and it sounded like harp chords flowing off his tongue. "It's just right. She's just right."

He smiled down at her, and in that time in space, everything truly was just right.

Chapter Seven

FOG HUNG LIKE a thick shawl over the hospital parking lot. The valet attendant zigzagged between cars, found Lindsey's, and pulled it out of the tight parking space. Damien would be back to the hospital before she woke. They had a baby and nothing at the cottage was prepared for her. Lindsey had a baby—but watching the birth had been so powerful and incredible, he had been part of it, too. He tipped the attendant and slid behind the wheel of Lindsey's car.

Something had loosened and stirred inside him as he looked at Maris's tiny face. He stole a few private moments with her in the dead of night as Lindsey slept, and cherished them. After the intensity of labor, he hadn't wanted to wake Lindsey right away. Damien had slipped the baby gingerly from the hospital bassinet. He made sure to hold her head, just like the nurse had instructed the day before, and sat in the rocker by the window. He'd pressed his lips to her forehead, and her downy hair tickled his chin. He loved her light powdery scent and the way her fingers wrapped around his.

Somehow, he'd started imagining they were both his; mother and baby. Everything he vowed he would never want had snuck up and wrapped itself tightly around his heart like vines of ivy creeping up a stone wall.

He drove toward the outskirts of Barnstable County where his GPS promised he'd find a baby supply store. When he reached the shopping plaza, he put the car in park and grabbed a cart. He figured he'd need it—they barely had anything for the baby—*she* barely had anything. Not they. The doors to the store automatically slid open when he approached and he stood there dumbfounded. A sea of endless aisles ran in straight lines under rows of fluorescent lights. Why did he think he could do this? He had no idea what a baby needed.

"Honey, you look a little lost. Can I help you find something?" A woman with silvery-white hair and a name tag that read Mary approached him.

"I could use some help," he admitted. "My…friend's baby made a surprise appearance. She needs it all."

She smiled and her brown eyes twinkled. "Well, you came to the right place. I think you might need an extra carriage, though." She grabbed one from the row outside the store. As she pushed her cart down aisle A, she said, "Let's start with the mama. Is she nursing or bottle feeding?"

"Nursing," Damien answered. He'd gone to get a coffee the night before when the lactation nurse had come to see how Lindsey was doing with feedings.

"She'd be grateful for this soothing cream then, and a special pillow to make feeding easier."

"Whatever you think is fine." Damien watched as the salesperson chose a salve and then hesitated at the pillows, which looked like half-eaten donuts.

"Boy or girl?" she asked with a hand hovering over the pillows.

"Girl." Damien moved closer to shelves. "This one will do." He chose the one with pink seahorses and shells.

"We have a bedding set and a mobile to match that," Mary said. Her silver hair brushed against her purple store shirt and her kind eyes sparkled, either with pity or delight over the commission she was about to earn.

Damien added both to the cart when they made it to the bedding and furniture aisle. The cart was quickly becoming close to full. He'd picked out onesies, hats, and swaddling blankets and Mary had helped him select diapers and rash cream. Now he stood debating over cribs. Had he ever imagined he'd be picking out a crib? He was probably overstepping his boundaries buying all this stuff, but the baby needed it, right? Lindsey and the baby would be in the hospital for a few days under observation—he wanted to surprise them with a nursery.

Mary walked over to the display beside him. "This crib is convertible." She trailed her fingers over the white curved rails. "It transitions to a toddler bed, then a daybed. The attached changing table will give you some extra space if the room is small."

The third bedroom was small, but the perfect size for a nursery. "This one's good," Damien said and flipped the price tag. He winced a bit. It wasn't like he didn't have the money; he'd spent years in the Marines, only touching his paychecks occasionally when on leave. What good was it doing just sitting there? If anyone deserved a surprise, it was Lindsey. He was sure she had thought of the baby's father as she powered through labor like a champion fighter. Damien had seen the pain radiate in her eyes, but she'd pushed through it. A new level of admiration had been layered onto the respect he had for her.

"All right, the last piece would be a rocker," Mary said and led him down another aisle in the seemingly endless store. "Now, it's not essential, but it's so nice and soothing to rock a baby to sleep."

Lindsey deserved a rocker, too. He knew she didn't have money to splurge on things, and he picked a tan-and-white glider with a matching ottoman. At checkout, he paid extra for next-day delivery. It would give him just enough time to paint before the furniture arrived. He tucked his debit card back into his wallet, pocketed the receipt, and pushed the consolidated cart into the lot. After loading the back of the car with shopping bags, Damien sparked the ignition, and backed out of the parking lot.

Salt marshes lined each side of the road. He left his windows rolled down, and the warm breeze hit his face carrying the scents of peat, salt water, and earth. He glanced out at the golden grass that speared up from a lacework of pools and streams. Damien had never really noticed how beautiful the landscape was growing up, but now that he returned as an adult, he could appreciate the little details. His plan was to drop the purchases off at the cottage, pick up sandwiches, and get back to Lindsey just in time for lunch. He did just that, making an additional stop in the hospital gift shop for an arrangement of flowers, with glittery pink alphabet blocks adorning it.

A smile burst over Lindsey's face when she saw them. Like the swift strike of a match, something lit inside Damien and burned straight through him. He was taken aback at his reaction. His feelings for her were intensifying and it scared the hell out of him. She was so pretty leaned back in the hospital bed, face serene and glowing. The sight of her always stole his breath. Steadier, he snuck over to her bedside, kissed her forehead, and placed the flowers on the nightstand.

"Damien—thank you." Her voice was filled with so much appreciation, it made him wonder when the last time was that someone had brought her flowers or had done something nice for her just because. It made him glad he'd snuck away early and faced the perils of the baby store.

"I think you'll be more thankful for this." He held up the takeout sack and her grin widened.

"You know me well. This hospital food just isn't cutting

it." She shifted to sit up and he tried not to look at her full breasts as the white sheet slipped revealing a thin-strapped top.

"And that pamphlet said you need extra calories for nursing." He pulled the sandwiches out of the bag and some potato salad. "There, just like a picnic." When he looked up, she was staring at him.

"You read pamphlets? On breastfeeding?" Lindsey raised her eyebrows at him.

"Yeah, it was in that folder they left you. I thought it might be helpful to scan through things." That was how he learned about baby proofing, and it served him well that morning when he chose outlet covers and cabinet locks.

"You surprise me, Damien." She offered him a saucy side smile that was a reward in itself.

"Well, your bunkmate should know a thing or two about babies if there's one in the house," he said and bit into his grinder. A thought popped into his head. Now that Maris was born, maybe Lindsey didn't want him under her roof. Her parents would eventually come home to visit and she'd have to explain why a man was living in her house.

"That is, if you're still okay with our arrangement." He leveled his eyes with hers and searched for any sign that she wasn't.

"It's nice having you around, Damien. The cottage has never looked better and I can't say the extra money doesn't help—especially now that Maris is born and I have nothing for her. I'll have to find a store to stop at before we get home." Worry clouded her eyes.

"Don't think about it now." He grasped her hand to distract her and glanced over at Maris, who was still sleeping soundly in the bassinet. "When you return to work, what will you do?"

"I'll have to find a day care and maybe when my parents are home from Aruba they'd be willing to take a few days. I'm just not sure I'll want to go back to the same type of job I had before. The hours are long, and I want to spend every moment I can with Maris." She took a sip of the apple juice sitting on her table.

"Why don't you paint?" he asked. Lindsey tensed up. She had always loved art and talent couldn't just poof into thin air, could it?

She shook her head. "I could never make enough from it. It's just a silly hobby." Lindsey twisted the straw in her drink.

Now he understood. "Did he tell you that?" He could see the answer in her eyes. "When we were young, you knew you'd grow up to be an artist. You have a special talent, Lindsey. Don't give that up."

"That's exactly it." She sighed. "We were young, with no worries or responsibilities. It's easy to dream big when you're not accountable for anything." Her words were true for her, but his childhood had been riddled with worry and responsibility. When he got home from school, would his father be passed out or waiting there with a belt? If he was really good and well behaved, his mother would come back and fix everything. But she hadn't and he was left to fend off his father on his own.

"I bet every single nautical shop would knock down the doors to buy your work. Tourists would eat up seaside paintings from a local artist with a spoon." Lindsey looked down at her lunch. Where was the spark of confidence she'd always had?

"I think you're overestimating my skills, Damien." She laughed it off and crumpled the empty sandwich wrapper.

They both whipped their heads around to the bassinet when Maris wailed. A smile broke over their faces and they giggled at their reaction.

"Stay there," Damien told Lindsey when she started to ease out of the bed. He walked over to the baby, lifted her carefully out of the bassinet, and placed her in Lindsey's arms. They made quite a picture snuggled together and again he longed to be part of that picture. He might enjoy playing house with Lindsey and the baby, but he couldn't stay here forever. His father's house had gone on the market and it was only a matter of time before it got snapped up. Real estate didn't sit long on the Cape. It would be easier for them both if he didn't get too attached. The problem was, he was already wrapped up in both of them.

Chapter Eight

MARIS SLEPT THE entire ride back to the cottage, securely fastened in the car seat that Damien had managed to purchase in-between hospital visits and caring for the dog. Lindsey would pay him back for it, as soon as she could get on her feet. He'd done so much for them. The tires crunched over the crushed seashell drive. Damien had brightened and sealed the shaker shingles, returning the cottage to a natural seaside gray and had painted the porch white. It looked just as she remembered it now. Tears stung her eyes—she was more sentimental now than when she was pregnant.

"Damien, it's beautiful." A lump lodged in her throat. She looked over and butterflies flapped in her belly when their eyes met. He reached over the center console and laced his fingers with hers. For one heartbeat, then two, they were connected with eyes locked and hands linked. She found more than just friendship in his deep blue eyes. There was an inexplicable need swimming in those stormy sapphire pools. His rough and callused hand felt so good against hers. She shivered when she thought of how they would feel running over her body. Then he broke away, leaving her longing for more contact.

"It's shaping up," he said in a voice that wasn't quite steady. He turned his head toward the backseat. "Can't believe she slept the whole way home."

"Me, either. It's kind of scary being away from the safety net of nurses and doctors." She glanced back at her baby, snoozing so peacefully. She loved the way her long lashes curved to her chubby cheeks.

"It did seem strange to just walk out of the hospital with something so precious. I figured you would've had to sign a waiver or something." He laughed softly.

They unloaded Maris, and Damien insisted on carrying the bags and the car seat. She could hear Daisy's whimpers and the click of her nails on the other side of the door. When Lindsey slid her key into the lock and opened it, the dog leaped out, her short tail happily ticking back and forth.

"I don't even know where to lay her down." Lindsey bit her bottom lip. She should have been more prepared, and now the baby was home and there wasn't a single thing for her.

"Come with me," Damien said in a low voice. The pace of her heart quickened. What did he have up his sleeve? Her breath caught and was trapped inside her throat when she looked through the opening of the third bedroom. Gratitude and wonder flooded through her, but when she opened her mouth to speak, nothing came out. She grasped his forearm with one hand and pressed the other to her mouth. All the tension she'd had over not being prepared seeped out of her. Damien had made her a dream nursery. The generosity and the scope of it floored her.

He'd painted the walls light pink and ruffled white curtains swayed in the windows, the warm salty breeze parting them slightly, bringing with it the fresh scent of the sea. A rocker sat in the corner, with a decorative seahorse pillow nestled against the arm. In the center of the room was a crib with delicately curved rails. A mobile that matched the rocker pillow spun slowly over the mattress; a parade of starfish and seahorses. Her eyes filled and overflowed. She didn't try to stop them. The thought he put into decorating the nursery was profound—no one had done anything so lavish or kind for her in all her life. It overwhelmed and humbled her. She laid Maris down on the mattress with its tightly fitted sheet, and turned to Damien.

This tough-as-nails man had selected the most feminine treasures to welcome her sweet baby into the world. She couldn't find the right words to express her gratitude.

"Damien—in my wildest dreams I couldn't have imagined a room so perfect. It might take a while, but I promise I'll repay you—for everything." She ran her fingers over the creamy curved rail of the crib.

He closed the gap between them, and ran a thumb over her cheek. "It's a gift, given without strings. I've never met anyone more deserving of something special."

Her body tingled with anticipation as he lowered his lips to hers. A wonderful heat melted through her heart. She wasn't sure how on earth he could find her attractive. She'd seen the dark circles sweeping under her eyes that morning. In fact, everything about her said tired and haggard, and her belly was still more than puffy. Damien didn't seem to care, as he pulled her in deeper. They jumped apart when the baby howled.

"Your chaperone's awake." He ran his hands down her arms, and a shiver coursed over her skin. "She seems to pick the most inopportune times to ask for her mama. Why don't you settle in? I'll rock her for a bit."

He didn't wait for her to answer, but simply bent over the crib and scooped up her daughter, then settled in the rocker by the window.

The sight of this brawny and rugged man holding her tiny little girl made her knees wobbly. Oh, how she wished there could be a future for them. One where Damien would come to love the town he hated so vehemently. One where he would move into the cottage, into her bed, and intertwine his hopes and dreams with hers. A simple life in Chatham wasn't his dream, though, and she wouldn't try to persuade him otherwise. It would only spawn resentment over time, if she tried to convince him to stay. She'd cherish the time they had now, and deal with the consequences and hurt when he left.

Lindsey longed for a hot shower and turned the knob

until a steamy spray churned out. She stepped in, tilted her head back under the warm water, and sighed. There was something to be said for being in your own space. She stayed there for a few moments, letting the soothing stream flow over her, and ease the aches and pains from labor. Her mind drifted to Damien. He'd been there for her when no one else had; not only to encourage her through the birth but afterward, too.

She knew he could have left at any time—a hotel room was bound to be open at this point, and yet he stayed. They had fallen into an easy rhythm, as the bond between them grew stronger. Lindsey lathered shampoo in her hair and the scent of vanilla and toasted coconut filled the room. She was just rinsing the soap off her skin when she heard the faint chime of the doorbell. Lindsey turned off the water and listened. Sure enough, it sounded again. Who would be visiting them? She quickly pulled on a thick bathrobe, wound her hair into a bun on the top of her head, and padded down the hall barefoot to the front door.

Damien was already standing there—face-to-face with her parents. She could see their confused expressions from over Damien's shoulder. Lindsey hadn't mentioned to them that a man was living with her, and now they were here, and she was in her bathrobe with Damien holding Maris. She could only imagine what they were thinking. Her cheeks heated.

"Mom, Dad, I thought you'd call first." She rushed over.

"You remember Damien, right? We went to school together."

"Yes." Her Father's brow creased and Lindsey's stomach sank. For Pete's sake, she was an adult; he couldn't ground her for having a boarder—but Damien had become more than that, so much more. She had come to count on him and enjoy his company. She liked sitting at the table with him and sharing a meal, or watching the waves roll in from the ocean on the deck. His kisses had sparked something deep inside her. Something she had never felt before—even during the good times with Matthew.

Damien stepped back so Lindsey could move forward. She kissed her father, Allen, on the cheek, breathing in his familiar aftershave, and then she hugged her mother, Tanya, and invited them inside. Tanya peered at Maris who was sleeping soundly in Damien's strong and capable arms.

"Oh, she's so lovely." Tanya clasped her hands together. "Congratulations, honey." She draped an arm over Lindsey's shoulder. "It was so nice of you to visit, Damien, to let Lindsey get settled."

Her father, who was traditional and old-fashioned in every way, loomed behind them. "We were sorry to hear about your father, son. Do you plan to move home?"

"I'm only passing through," Damien said and Lindsey's heart sank. Did the weighty disappointment show on her face? "I just came home to wrap up some loose ends." His body swayed back and forth slightly as he rocked the baby.

"So, you're staying in town then, or your dad's place?" Allen pried. Why couldn't he just drop it?

"No." Damien met her father's hard stare, unfazed by the sharp tone in his voice. "I'm staying right here."

The room went silent and the warmth in Lindsey's cheeks rushed to her ears. "Let's go sit in the living room, and you'll want to see the baby's nursery, too." She had to change the subject, and walked down the hall. Lindsey's eyes flicked up to the ceiling and she silently said thanks when she heard footsteps behind her.

"Just look at it, Allen," Tanya said when they reached Maris's room. "It's like a magazine picture. So sweet and tasteful." At least they approved of the nursery—the one Damien had designed. If they'd come two weeks earlier, the cottage would still be an utter disaster. She owed Damien—big-time.

She wasn't sure she should reveal that Damien had single-handedly orchestrated the masterpiece when they were still wrapping their heads around the fact that he lived in the cottage with her. Lindsey ushered them into the living room.

"Would either of you like a drink? I'm afraid there's not much in the house right now." Lindsey pushed aside some of the boxes that were left from sorting through papers the day she went into labor.

"Water would be fine, dear." Tanya settled down on the couch. Lindsey started to walk toward the kitchen and Damien stopped her.

"You relax. I'll get it." He waited for her to sit down and then placed Maris into her arms. When he returned, he carried three iced waters on a tray and placed it on the coffee table.

"I have a few things I need to take care of in town," he announced. "It was nice to see you both," he said to her parents. Then he did the unexpected. He leaned down and kissed her forehead, then the baby's. The gesture of possession surprised her. Even though her parents were looking on slack-jawed, little wings sprouted on her heart and fluttered happily.

"Can I get you anything while I'm out?" he whispered and his breath tickled her ear.

"That's okay, thanks." She smiled.

"I'll bring home dinner. You take it easy." He held her gaze and brushed his thumb over her cheek. He was making his position loud and clear. She swallowed hard. Lindsey was going to get an earful when he left.

It was only under the watchful eye of her parents that she realized just how domestic they'd become. When the front door closed, her parents turned toward her.

"Lindsey." She cringed at her father's disapproving tone. "What's going on? You just signed divorce papers and now you've invited Damien to live with you?" He shook his head. "I don't understand it. Matthew was a good provider—is that why you left him? For Damien?" He said his name like it was poison on his tongue.

Her father had been partial to Matthew because he came from a good family, dressed the part of a proper gentleman, and said all the right things. Embarrassment had stopped her from telling them the real reason she had left her husband. When he cheated, she'd felt partially responsible—like maybe if she had been a better wife, he wouldn't have strayed. Now, it made her wonder if she'd be enough for Damien. How could she convince him to stay when she couldn't even keep her husband by her side?

"I just struggled through labor and Damien was there for me. Do you see Matthew anywhere?" she questioned in a biting tone that surprised even her. "That's because he threw me and his baby aside, so he and his secretary could start fresh." She held the baby tighter and heat spread over her scalp like a thousand fire ants skittering through her hair. She didn't wait for any replies before she bulldozed on.

"That nursery you saw? Damien designed it while I was in the hospital. He installed the car seat and picked us up. He's spent the past three days readying the house for Maris and me, and taking care of Daisy."

"Honey, I wish you'd told us about Matthew. I'm glad you had Damien here. I'll forever feel guilty for missing the birth." Her mother rubbed her hand over her arm while her father crossed his tightly across his chest. Tanya had always been quick to accept Lindsey's choices. She was so thankful for it.

"He drives a motorcycle. He's covered in tattoos. He

comes from the most dysfunctional family in town." Her father's forehead creased as he stared her down. Lindsey blew out a breath. This was ridiculous. She was an adult for crying out loud.

"Those tattoos represent his time in the Marines, and for his friend who died overseas." She'd asked him about the infantry badge on his shoulder with the words "Semper Fi" below it, and the single eagle wing across his shoulder with a date and initials. "Yes, his family situation was unthinkable, but you can't blame him for the actions of his parents."

"Allen," her mother snapped. "Drop it. Let's enjoy our grandchild." Lindsey was thankful for her intervention and she passed Maris into her eager arms. Daisy immediately jumped onto the couch and snuggled into her lap where the baby had been sitting. Sibling jealously was already starting for her poor little dog.

They spent the next hour talking about her parents' most recent trip to their timeshare in Aruba, the baby, and the cottage—all carefully avoiding the topic of Damien. She was disappointed in her father's disapproval, but she could understand that his concern came from a place of love. When they finally left to go home, she closed the door behind them, and leaned her back against the door. She had never been so grateful for solitude in her life.

She carried Maris into the nursery and settled down in the rocker, slowly swaying back and forth as the baby nursed. Every time she entered the room she thought of all Damien had done for her. It was the reason her father's reaction to him angered her so. Damien was a good man; dependable and stable, rugged and kind. And heart thumping, knees weakening, dizzingly attractive. The combination of both was sucking her heart into a vortex of feeling. It would be impossible to ignore the pull of it, dragging her closer and closer to love—she'd never be able to crawl out of the forceful spin of sensations barreling through her.

She hoped her parents' less-than-warm welcome hadn't made him question what he was doing with her. Damien had gone to give them time alone, but she wished he had stayed. Black clouds were billowing over the horizon and the rolling, choppy waves meant a storm was coming.

Chapter Nine

DAMIEN WATCHED THE same dark clouds build and spread over the sky, and hoped the takeout order was prepared fast. He wanted to get home to Lindsey and the baby before the storm crashed down on the shoreline. The drifter in him said to stop playing house with her and move on, but there was another, more grounded, part that wanted desperately to stay. He took one of the few empty seats at the bar and ordered a soda. Having Lindsey and Maris to get home to made him cautious. The restaurant was bustling with locals catching the ball game, and tourists who came to sample the Italian fare Anthony's offered. The TV mounted behind the bar was barely audible over the chatter of the crowd.

His mind wandered back to that afternoon. Lindsey's parents had been surprised to see him. He couldn't blame them; he wasn't what he'd want for his daughter, either. It didn't matter. He was dating Lindsey, not her parents. His brows knitted together. Is that what they were doing? Dating? Despite not taking her on a proper "date," he supposed they had become more than just friends. The problem was, Lindsey's life was here on the Cape and his was anywhere else.

The bartender returned and placed a glass in front of him. He drank deeply, rested his arms on the glossy wood bar, and tuned in halfheartedly to the baseball game. In the corner of his eye, he caught a blur as someone moved close to him.

"Hey, brother." Damien turned as a man grabbed the barstool to his left. One side of his face was youthful and unlined, while the other was marred with deep burns. The only thing similar on both sides of his face was cheerful brown eyes and a friendly smile. The innocent look reminded him of Johnny. The man held out his hand to Damien.

"Twelfth Marine Regiment. I saw your tat from across the bar. My name's Jay." Damien met his hand and shook.

"Damien." He motioned to the bartender. "What are you drinking?"

"The summer ale on tap," Jay said. "Are you on leave?" he added after the bartender slid an empty glass from the rack, filled it, and placed it on a napkin in front of him.

"No. I'm done." When Jay continued to stare at him, he elaborated. "I was on active duty for nine years. When my last contract lapsed I decided it was time to move on. Now I'm trying to figure out what to do with my time. You?" Damien took a drink from his glass.

"IED took some of my sight." Jay lowered his drink and looked at Damien. "I received an honorable discharge."

Damien nodded. He understood the struggle. "Are you able to work, now that you're home?"

"For a while, I had a tough time of it, but I moved here and got hooked up with Veterans' Services." Jay took a long pull from his beer.

"That's good. Some buddies of mine had a real problem transitioning home. There seemed to be a lack of services to help them with it." He had worked hard, too, to overcome the constant nightmares and the feeling that he was completely alone.

"That's just the thing. For a long time, I didn't know where to turn. Then Veterans' Services showed me there are a lot of government programs available to military families that many people aren't aware of. We get them the help they need, so they can start a good civilian life." Jay reached his hand down, pulled his wallet out of his pant pocket, and opened the distressed leather case.

"Here's my card. You should stop by sometime. It's a great organization and we have some open positions if you're looking for something in the area." Jay drained his beer and left some bills on the table. "I'm sitting over there with some vets from the office. Come over if you feel like it."

Right on cue a server breezed through the door to the kitchen, carrying a plastic bag for Damien. It wasn't that he didn't appreciate Jay's offer—he might have kicked back a few with fellow veterans under different circumstances, but he really wanted to get home to Lindsey and Maris.

"Thanks, but my friend just had a baby. I'm bringing some provisions," he said holding up the bag.

"Congrats. I'll keep my eye out at the office for you." He clapped a hand on Damien's back and strode to the corner table where he came from.

The clouds that hung at the horizon when he entered the restaurant now rolled overhead. A strong gust of wind whipped at his T-shirt, and he wished for Lindsey's car. He got on his bike and hoped for the best, but the black clouds above hinted toward a wild and wet ride. The rain held until he pulled into the driveway of the cottage and then it started pelting down in thick sheets. He raced to the door, greeted Daisy, and turned the oven on low. Damien transferred the chicken and pasta to a casserole dish and set it inside to warm.

The house was quiet and dark. He tiptoed down the hall, because somewhere in the cottage was a tiny sleeping angel that turned into a beast when awakened. He found mother and baby asleep in the rocker. They made a picture, one that tugged at his heart. Lindsey's head drooped slightly so that her check rested lightly on the baby's hair. Maris had her head angled toward her mother's chest. Damien knelt beside them and just watched for a moment. What was he going to do about these feelings ballooning inside him? Seeing them added a happy light to his days, and a joy he didn't know he could feel again after seeing so much dark, so much pain.

It was more than want, he was sure of it. He'd had women before and never felt an ounce of the affection he felt toward Lindsey. Maybe it was because every other woman paled in comparison to her. Because physically, the jolt of their first unsteady and clumsy kiss when they were kids overpowered everything he experienced after—like having sponge cake after tasting crème brûlée.

It was the first kiss that made him pull away from her and the friendship they'd forged. And why? At the time, he had convinced himself he was doing her a favor by backing away. She was out of his league in every sense. Lindsey came from a respected family, was popular, and had good grades. Damien ran with the wrong crowd, scraped by in school, and his home life had been a train wreck. Now he could see that those were excuses—they were justified, but excuses all the same. He'd been afraid of getting too close, of caring too much, because the one person who had truly got him, the person who had given him life, and was supposed to cherish him above all else, had left. He always wondered if there was something wrong with him—something that made her leave. If he and Lindsey got involved, part of him was terrified that she'd leave him, too, just like his mother.

Lindsey stirred and murmured something in her sleep. He indulged himself by stroking his hand down her silken hair. If he could have all this, would staying in Chatham be such a terrible thing after all? Perhaps the constant reminders of his sad childhood could be replaced by something bright and beautiful with Lindsey and Maris. Lindsey's eyes fluttered, then popped open.

"I didn't mean to fall asleep with her in the chair," she said. "It's not safe to do that." Her eyes were heavy from sleep, and so alluring.

"She's all right and swaddled up close to you." He ran a finger over the baby's cozy blanket. Lindsey jumped when lightning flashed outside and thunder cracked overhead.

"Whoa. Can't believe I was sleeping through that." She angled her head to peek out the window.

"It's bad out there. I just made it into the driveway when the sky opened up. I got dinner—whenever you're ready."

"I'll lay Maris down. She might sleep through the storm," she said.

Lindsey moved the baby away from her, exposing a perfectly rounded breast. Heat spread through him, and he got up to give her some privacy. Lindsey needed time to heal and recuperate from childbirth. Sex had to be the absolute furthest thing from her mind right now, and that was just fine. The saying was right; the best things were worth waiting for. Besides, he could show her how much he wanted to be part of her life in other ways, like shouldering some of the house work while she got some much-needed sleep. Damien inhaled through his nose and filled his lungs. He was seriously considering the possibility of staying.

He had set the table, poured drinks, and plated the food when Lindsey appeared. She'd tossed on a sweater that draped over her hips. He swallowed hard, she looked good with the soft material hugging her curves. Lightening illuminated the room and they both waited for the boom of thunder that followed. The dog whimpered and cowered under the kitchen table. Once they were both settled, Lindsey reached across the table and covered his hand with hers.

"When my parents visited today, I realized just how much you've been doing to help me. It's been more than just preparing the nursery and fixing the cottage. You wash the dishes and pick up around here. You take Daisy for walks in the morning. Things have changed between us, and I don't want you paying to stay anymore." She squeezed his hand and searched his face.

"When your parents stopped by, it opened my eyes to some things, too." He laced his fingers with hers, intertwining them. "I don't want to be your boarder and I don't want to be some friend passing through." Her shoulders sank and she glanced down at the table. "Lindsey." He spoke her name softly and she looked up at him. "I want more. What we have—it's something different, something special. We would be cheating ourselves if we didn't explore exactly what that could be."

He could tell she wanted to as well even before she opened her mouth to speak. Something lit in her eyes, happiness? Hope?

"Damien." She laughed out a breath. "I've wanted that since that night we were paired up in Spin the Bottle."

"I did, too." He'd wanted her with a force close to gravity. Just as he wanted her now.

"Then why did you push me away?" She tilted her head and took a sip of her drink.

"The kiss—or what I felt from it—was too much. Everything was such a mess then. I couldn't drag you into that." Damien smirked at her to lighten the mood. "Besides, what would your parents have thought then if their daughter, the town sweetheart with the world at her fingertips, was dating the likes of me?"

Lindsey scoffed. "Don't sell yourself short. I wanted you. That's what should have mattered. And town sweetheart? That's not how people saw me, Damien."

"It's how I saw you," he murmured. "Sometimes I'd come to the football games and stand near the bleachers to see you cheer." Her long, tanned legs and thigh-high red skirt had fueled most of his adolescent fantasies. "Still have that uniform?" He grinned.

"It wouldn't cover half of my backside now—so no, the uniform is out of commission."

"You wouldn't find me complaining." He loved the way her eyes lightened playfully when he joked with her.

"In all seriousness," she said, "I think we should set some ground rules."

"Okay, then. What are the rules?" Damien matched her thoughtful tone. He picked up his fork and twirled some pasta around it.

"We take things slowly—day by day. If either of us feels it's not working, we end things as friends. And when your father's house sells, you'll give me fair warning before you leave."

"Why are you so sure I'll leave, Lindsey?" Her eyes shot up from her plate.

"You're considering staying? Damien—you've hated this town ever since we were kids."

"I've been seeing it in a different light lately." He sent her a long look. Did she understand it was her and Maris that had changed the filter on his lens?

She stared at him for a long moment. "Why?"

"You chase away the shadows, and then Maris fills that space with light. I'm honest-to-God happy, and it has everything to do with you and that sweet baby." He rubbed his thumb over her knuckles, and she blinked quickly a few times.

"Maybe everything we've gone through has been a stepping stone to bring us back together." Lindsey's voice was a delicate whisper but her words rocked him like the sea.

AFTER THEY ATE and put the dishes in the sink, Lindsey went down the hall to look in on the baby who was still sleeping soundly. Damien walked up behind her and kneaded her shoulders lightly.

"You should try to sleep while she is. It's only a matter of time before the first late night feeding." His breath caught when she turned into him.

"Come with me?" Goose bumps popped over his skin when her breath tickled his neck. When a bolt of lightning lit the dark hallway, he could see the desire in her eyes.

"It's too soon. The doctor said it could take six weeks for you to feel back to normal. I don't want to hurt you, Lindsey."

"It seems like so long but it's definitely too soon." She ran her hands up his chest and his body reacted to her instantly.

"I can wait." His voice was low and gruff. "For now, we can just cuddle." He followed Lindsey into her bedroom, and climbed into bed beside her. The rain beating against the windows made the space seem like a warm cocoon. She snuggled up close to him. Damien circled his hand up and down her back and she arched up and kissed his chin. He angled his face to meet her lips—petal-soft and wanting.

The kiss started slow and sweet but it didn't stay that way for long. Her hands were under his shirt, his were tangled in her hair. Their breath turned to fast pants and he pulled her hips into his. She pushed against him in a tantalizing rhythm, making the longing unbearable. His hands roamed over her shirt and a throb ebbed through him when they passed over her nipples, taut and hard against the cotton fabric of her shirt. When she groaned, he cupped his hands there and let his thumbs circle slowly. She pushed away and sat up suddenly. He followed her eyes down the twin spots that had soaked through her shirt.

She laughed and let out a sigh. "Nothing like some breast milk to ruin a sexy moment." She climbed over him and returned wearing a clean shirt. This time when she nestled in his arms, he kept his body still and his hands firmly wrapped around her. He tried to ignore the tingles he got when her fingertips traced lightly over his sides. When they passed over his scars, her calm green eyes joined with his.

"Will you tell me what happened?" she whispered. He hadn't talked about it to anyone outside the regiment, but Lindsey was staring at him with open and trustworthy eyes. His heartbeat thrummed a little faster, as it did every time he relived the moments.

He nodded and took a breath. "As a sniper, I had a spotter. Someone who covered me while I was focused on the targets. His name was Johnny. A young kid from the South who desperately wanted the college education the military offered. We went through basic training together and became fast friends. It was hard not to—everyone loved him. He was quick to joke and always made light of things when we were caked in layers of dust and sand."

"He sounds like a really great person," Lindsey said softly. Her hands had stopped running up and down his skin and she focused her eyes intently on his.

He pulled in a shaky breath, and then continued. "We

were on a standard mission. I remember he was looking forward to heading back to base for dinner. They were making chili that night and Johnny loved it. He always said his mother wasn't much of a cook. Must not have been because the food was God-awful. We got ambushed from behind and he was shot. Before I could get to him, a grenade went off. I remember the explosion, then the ringing in my ears. Everything was in slow motion, then the world went black. I woke up in the hospital and Johnny didn't wake up at all." Her hands rubbed his arms.

"Oh, Damien. I'm so sorry." She wrapped him in a hug and pressed her lips to his chest.

"I picked the spot that day. He thought we should've gone farther—and if we had…"

"Damien, you can't blame yourself. It will eat you up inside. He wouldn't want you to carry such a heavy burden."

"No, he wouldn't," Damien admitted. His friend had been as light-hearted and kind as it gets. He hadn't deserved to die that day. He pulled his eyes shut for a moment, and tried to shake the memories away.

They talked for a while longer, and he took comfort in the sound of her voice. It didn't take long for her eyelids to grow heavy and her breathing to deepen. He pushed away a lock of hair that had fallen in front of her face and enjoyed the scent of the shampoo she always used that clung to it. With the pitter-patter of rain against the roof, he took a moment to really look at her. A thick fringe of lashes lay flush against her creamy skin. A rosy blush swept over her high cheekbones, and led down to full lips. He kissed her forehead and hugged her tightly.

He was thrilled she wanted more from their relationship and filled with hope over what they could make of it. Damien tried to steady the part of him that instinctively whispered to run far and fast. Deep down he was scared as hell that things wouldn't work out, and he'd lose her twice. This time around, he'd do everything in his power to be the man she saw him as—the man she deserved. He thought back to the card Jay had handed him at the bar. Maybe it was time to explore his options and see what types of positions were available on the Cape. Could he really turn the tides and make Chatham his home again? He looked down at Lindsey. It was definitely worth a try.

Chapter Ten

WHEN MARIS WENT down for a nap, Lindsey took her easel onto the deck and faced the water. She added cobalt-blue paint to her pallet and set the tube beside her. Ever since Damien mentioned her paintings, she had an itch to pull out her oils and transform a blank canvas into its own little world. Lindsey recalled the peace she felt as a teenager when she sat at her easel. All her problems seemed to melt away when she was face-to-face with a creamy white canvas and the smell of turpentine in the air. At the time, those problems had been a sliver of those she dealt with in adulthood—grades and test scores, boys and prom dates. Her lips curved. If only things could be so easy now.

She swept her brush through the thick oil paint and watched as a sea gull dove into the water after its prey. Lindsey could paint the rolling sea of Chatham from memory, along with the rocky jetties that projected from the land into the water, and the stately white-washed lighthouses that called ships home.

Damien's suggestion of selling her work had nagged at her since he'd mentioned it at the hospital. She finally unearthed some old paintings she'd done of the shoreline and stacked them in her bedroom. After walking by them for weeks, she was finally compelled to try her hand at it again. Damien inspired her, and lit a fire deep within her to explore all that life had to offer. Painting had once been her greatest dream. She arched the brush over the canvas, and let the call of the gulls and the sound of the waves relax her.

Lindsey was embarrassed at how quickly she'd put art aside when Matthew scoffed at her longing to be a painter. She had bended to him too easily, desperately trying to make the marriage work. Thankfully, it hadn't worked because now she understood his need to control, to possess. They had never been equals. They were never a team. Like she and Damien were, she thought. They shared everything. The household chores, time with Maris, their hopes and dreams—but they still hadn't had sex. They curled up in the same bed together every night and his kisses and touches drove her mad—but he didn't push for more. Was he still giving her space to recover, or was something else holding him back? If there wasn't such fire in his eyes, such passion when their lips met, she would wonder if he found her desirable at all.

She mixed some yellow paint onto her brush, and started scrubbing light into a wave breaking over the beach. She wanted so much to believe their relationship could work for the long haul, but insecurities whispered in her ear. Would he truly stay when his father's house sold, or would the lure to travel off the Cape be too strong to resist? Lindsey picked up her palette knife, pulled it through burnt sienna, and scraped a jetty into the water. She was so in tune with her work and with the sounds of nature around her, she didn't hear the screen door open.

She jumped and nearly dropped her tools when Damien spoke behind her.

"That's something else, Lindsey." He leaned down and kissed the top of her head. "I didn't mean to startle you."

She turned and smiled when she saw Maris in his arms and the dog prancing at his feet. She'd never tire of the twirl of happiness that circled through her at the sight of them together.

"Would you mind if Maris and I took your car? We have an errand to run."

She raised her brow. "It's a little early for driving lessons." Lindsey knew Damien was perfectly capable of strapping Maris in her car seat and keeping her safe. He'd had as much of a hand in raising her as she did. "If you give me half an hour, I could go, too."

"No, keep at it." He motioned toward her painting. "We won't be long and when I get back you and I are going on a date." Damien cooed softly to the baby when she started to fuss. Had a man ever been more beautiful?

Lindsey laughed. "Yeah, right. Who'll watch Maris?"

"Your parents. They seemed over the moon when I asked them yesterday." He shifted Maris to his other side, looking completely confident and competent with the little baby in his arms. Damien had become very domestic in a short period of time. He grabbed her chin with his free hand and planted a kiss on her lips. "We have something to celebrate." His eyes danced with mischief.

"We do? What do you have up your sleeve?" Lindsey narrowed her eyes at him, got up from her seat, and kissed Maris on her forehead.

"You'll see." He grinned. "We should be back by five and your parents will be here around six." Damien pecked her cheek and breezed back through the sliding glass door.

What was he up to? She finished her painting and went straight for the shower. A thought shook her as she soaped up. The house must have sold. She caught her bottom lip between her teeth. What would happen now? A sick churning looped in her stomach. If the house was gone, he was no longer tied to Chatham. She tried to push it aside and just get ready for their date. Lindsey rolled her shoulders and tried to loosen the tension that rested between them. She ran her fingers over her wet hair, and wrung out the excess water. They'd seen each other every day for weeks. Why was she so nervous?

Lindsey pulled out all the stops, enhancing her eyes with mascara and turning her lips into a sultry slick pout with lipstick and gloss. She used a round brush and blow dryer to add some extra oomph to her straight hair. Her room looked as though a hurricane blew through it as she rummaged through her closet, tossing articles of clothing all over the bed until she found something that satisfied her. Lindsey let out a grateful breath when the zipper on the black dress pulled up easily.

She was just clasping a silver pendant around her neck w the side door opened. Lindsey hoped she hadn't gone overboard but it was her first date in a very, very long time, with a man who put stars in her eyes and a song in her heart. He stopped dead in his tracks when he saw her in the hallway, Maris in one hand, and a lush bouquet of pink peonies in the other.

"I don't tell you enough, Lindsey, but you're beautiful. It doesn't matter if you're in sweatpants or dressed up, you're striking."

It wasn't his kind words that had her heart jumping to her throat, but the intense look in his eyes that told her he meant every word of it.

"For my date," he said holding out the bouquet. "Every head will turn tonight when you walk by."

She moved closer, accepted the flowers, and inhaled their sweet scent. She lifted her gaze to him and for one heartbeat, their eyes locked. The air around them sparked with electricity. Eager anticipation danced in the space between them. They both looked up at the sound of a knock on the door—a distinct rat-a-tat-tat. Why did her parents always have to be early? She was disappointed the moment ended and went to open the door for them.

"Where's that little munchkin?" her mother said and gave her a quick hug before breezing past. Her father followed her inside, and glanced with approval at the flowers she held. After a few family dinners together, he'd thawed to the idea of Damien. She secretly thought he even liked him. Her dad kissed her cheek and walked over to Maris, who was being smothered with nuzzles and coos.

"We were starting to think you'd never ask us to babysit," Tanya said, and easily stole Maris from Damien's arms.

Lindsey started rattling off instructions and feeding habits and she pointed out the list of important numbers that hung on the fridge.

"Don't you worry." Allen raised his brows at the instructions. "We managed to keep you alive, didn't we?"

Lindsey laughed. "That doesn't inspire much confidence, Dad." She took a deep breath. It would be their first time leaving the house without Maris.

Tanya rolled her eyes. "It shouldn't." She turned toward Damien and added, "I left one afternoon to go shopping and came home to Lindsey munching on crayons. Allen was fast asleep and the house looked as though a tornado swept through."

Allen's eyes twinkled. "Fathering is tiring business." He chuckled.

"You two get going and don't worry about a thing. We've got this." Tanya grinned and planted a kiss on the baby's cheek.

"Okay, but just call if—" Lindsey started to say.

"We will. We'll call with any questions. Just go and have a nice time." Allen put a hand on his wife's shoulder and began to lead her into the living room.

Damien took Lindsey's keys off the counter, and placed a hand at the small of her back as they walked toward the driveway. He opened the door for her, and closed it once she was settled inside.

"What's all this about, Damien? You're being very secretive." She grinned even though nerves swam through her stomach like minnows pushing against a net.

"Just relax and enjoy. When's the last time you went out for a nice night?" He started the car, glanced over, and smirked back. He was definitely up to something.

"Hmm." She tried to think back. "I guess if I have to think about it this long, it's been a while. What about you?"

"My feet barely touched U.S. soil before I found out my father died. After that, I was on the road to come here. The last time I went out and really enjoyed it was that morning we went to the diner. It's when you decided to let me bunk at your house." His lips curved.

"It was a very smart decision." She looked out to the water as they drove past a stretch of beach. Straggling beachgoers were pulling down their colorful umbrellas and folding up sandy towels. "You've more than upheld your end of our bargain. I still have a stack of papers to go through."

She really needed to get on it. It wasn't fair to slack on her end of the deal when he'd completed his in spades.

"There's no rush." He turned the wheel, and they pulled up to a waterside restaurant.

Lights glowed from every window and patrons meandered along the elegant wraparound porch, enjoying the ocean view. Damien came around to her side of the car, opened the door, and together they walked under the white columned portico and into the restaurant. He had put a lot of thought into this. More flutters filled her chest. The hostess found their name in her book, took two menus, and led them to a corner table. The wide arched windows opened the room up to the ocean.

"This view is incredible. It's like we're right on the beach." Lindsey looked out and memorized the landscape. The sun was beginning to dip lower over the horizon. The sky looked like rainbow sherbet with wispy, cotton candy-pink clouds surrounding a ripe orange sun that cast a trail of vanilla sparkles over the calm water.

"Looks like we'll catch the sunset from here, too." He reached across the table and took her hand. The small gesture still sent tingles down her spine, especially when he caressed her hand, like she was something precious and dear to him. Even though it was wrong, part of her desperately hoped his father's house stayed on the market for a little longer. The other part of her wished only good things for him—even if it meant he chose to leave after all. The waitress visited their table, took their drink order, and returned quickly with two frosty glasses of lemonade. Lindsey would be nursing for a while yet so the long list of high-end wines was off-limits.

The menu had her mouth watering and in the end, she decided on seared sea scallops, while Damien ordered a steak. Once the waitress left with their order, Damien met her eyes and smiled. He had a face she'd never tire of seeing, and the curve at his lips made her heart croon—like she was the motive for it.

"Now, for the reason behind our celebration." He gave her hand a quick squeeze and dug into his pocket. Her heart leaped into her throat and returned to her chest when he pulled out an envelope and set it next to him. She had to laugh at herself. What was she expecting—a ring? They'd reconnected only a few months ago. Their future was so uncertain. How could she possibly think that? Is that what she wanted from him? To be tangled up in another marriage? It was a scary thought, but Damien made her want those things again—the promises and the responsibility of them.

"I know you've been saying you don't think your talent could earn you a livable income, so when you pulled out those old oil paintings, I borrowed one and took it to the gallery on Main Street—just to see." His smile grew wider, as the corners of her lips dropped.

Her eyes narrowed. How could he think it was okay to take one of her paintings, to make that kind of decision on her behalf? Anger simmered slowly under the surface of her skin.

As if reading her mind, he squeezed her hand. "Linds, I believe in you. I know I didn't ask to take the canvas but I wanted to show you how talented you really are. To make you have confidence in yourself just like I do." Damien straightened out the envelope on the table.

"I'm trying hard to build my confidence back up on my own, and part of that step would have been soliciting my work when the time was right." Lindsey balled her hands into tight fists in her lap. "You have no idea what it was like with Matthew. He made every decision. Dictated every choice. He made me feel like…like I was never enough."

Matthew had been all about control, always telling her how to wear her hair and how to dress. He made sure they socialized with the right circle to fuel his career, and brushed off the idea of meeting the friends she'd made in college. Damien was supposed to understand her better than anyone—and yet hadn't he just taken control away from her, too?

Lindsey glanced down at the table. Her eyes burned with fresh tears fighting to escape over the edges of her eyelids. She forced them back, and looked up at Damien who sat dumbfounded, like a steamroller had just chugged through the dining room and flattened him.

When he spoke, his terse words were barely a whisper. "How could you say I have no idea what it's like to have control stripped away from me? To be made to feel less? My dad told me every day with his fists. No matter how good I was, no matter what I did right, I couldn't stop him. My mother wasn't there to protect me because I wasn't enough to make her stay."

His eyes bore into her with such ferocity, it was a wonder she didn't melt into a waxy puddle of guilt on the floor. Of course, he knew what it felt like, he'd had a whole lifetime of mental abuse and came out stronger for it. She'd put up with Matthew for only two years, and it crushed her. What did that say about the strength of her character? She looked down at the table, unable to hold his tense gaze.

"Lindsey, look at me." She brought her eyes up to his. "I submitted your painting because I believe in your talent. You're blowing it out of proportion. If you want to experience selling it to someone yourself, take it into another gallery."

Her back stiffened and she sat up straight as an iron rod. How could he downplay her feelings and tell her she was overreacting? Her feelings were hers, and hers alone.

"You believe in my talent, Damien, but not in me. Do you think I'll never be strong enough to develop the confidence to do things on my own?"

"That's not what I was thinking at all. I thought if you could sell your work, you'd be able to stand on your own two feet while doing what you love."

So that's what this was all about. He wanted her to stand

on her own, so he could hit the road like he'd always intend-
ed to. How silly she'd been to think their growing
relationship would be enough to keep him here. Well, he
could pack up and go at any time. She'd be just fine, financially and otherwise. It was a lie, one that hurt her so deeply.
She wouldn't be okay if he left.

Their meals came and they both sat in strained silence.
She could have been tasting the world's finest cuisine or a
pile of dirt. The fight had stripped her senses bare, and all
she could focus on was their crumbling relationship, falling
apart in a matter of moments, like an overbaked coffee cake.

They limped through a painfully quiet dinner. Damien
asked the waitress for the check, and slid his credit card
inside the leather pad without glancing at the bill. They left
the restaurant walking single file, like they were part of a
chain gang. The car ride was no better. Scenery blurred past
as they drove mile after mile without a single word. The
silence inside the car was deafening. This had been their first
real date, and it went up in flames faster than a dried-out log
soaked in gasoline. Was it a foreshadowing of their future?

When the car finally crawled into the driveway, Lindsey
unbuckled before Damien was able to shift gears into Park.
She couldn't stand another moment of the hushed disappointment that circled the air around them.

They walked in and found her parents watching televi-
sion.

"You're back early," Tanya said. "Did you have a nice

time?"

"Yes," Lindsey choked out. Of course, they knew otherwise. Damien and Lindsey stood feet away from each other, and her eyes were probably puffy from holding back the waterfall of tears that wanted to explode from her eyes. She noticed a look pass between her parents.

"Was Maris all right?" Lindsey fiddled with the fabric of her dress. If only everyone would just clear out and she could be alone.

"Good as gold." Her father flicked off the TV and stood up. Her mother followed his lead. They hugged her, said goodbye to Damien, and left quickly, sensing the unsettled air.

Lindsey went straight for the nursery and sunk into the rocker by Maris's crib. When she heard the door to Damien's room shut, she leaned her head back against the padded headrest. Maris was all she needed. She breathed in her soft new scent and let the tears flow down her cheeks. It seemed like things had ended before they'd even begun. She braced herself, knowing she might find him gone in the morning.

Chapter Eleven

WHEN DAMIEN WOKE the morning after his date with Lindsey, he rolled to his side and stared out the window. How had things gone so terribly wrong? He'd seriously pissed her off. Damien knew he shouldn't have taken the painting. If she'd only unsealed the letter instead of stubbornly tucking it away, her tune may have changed. He considered leaving the night before, just to get some space and air. It only would've made matters worse.

The fact that he even thought about running away shook him. It made him remember who he could become—a coward who fled from his responsibilities, like his mother. He wouldn't ignore the problem, either, as his father would have. The need to be stronger than those he came from pushed him out of bed. He tugged on jeans and a black T-shirt, and went to find Lindsey. They'd deal with their issues, head-on.

Hairs prickled up on his arms when he didn't find them in the house. Wouldn't that be something, if they were the ones to leave? His stomach clenched, then released, when he saw Lindsey sitting at the water's edge with Maris on her lap and Daisy chasing the tide in and out. The dog barked every so often when the water lapped at her feet. He strode down to them, picking up a few flat rocks as he went. She didn't turn to look at him when he approached, just gazed out blankly over the horizon.

He sat down in a sandy pocket next to her, and held out some of the rocks, like a peace offering.

"Best out of three?" He looked her in the eyes, hoping to disarm her.

"Might be kind of tough to skip rocks." Lindsey motioned to Maris who was wide-eyed and awake. Her eyes had changed from newborn-blue to Lindsey's sea-glass green.

"I wanted to talk to you about last night," he said. When Lindsey didn't respond, he continued. "I'm sorry, Lindsey. I am. I never meant to upset you or take away control. I was just…trying to make you happy, I guess, but I didn't think things all the way through."

"You want me to stand on my own two feet, I know that. Tell me honestly, is that why you've stayed here so long? Because you're afraid of what will happen to me if you leave? That I won't be able to care for myself and Maris?"

He put down the rocks and splayed his hands out on the sand. Damien's stomach was hard and tight, like someone had emptied a bucket of concrete into it.

"Lindsey, that's not it at all. There was something else I wanted to talk to you about last night, but it wasn't the right time." She shifted Maris in her arms, then looked up, waiting for him to continue. "The night your parents came home from Aruba, I met a guy who works for Veteran's Services, while I was picking up takeout at Anthony's. He told me there were positions available in town to help military families, and we've talked a few times since then. When he originally brought up work, the timing wasn't right. I think it is now."

Lindsey seemed to hesitate and he wondered if she wanted him to put down roots at all. "Is it something you'd be interested in? Something you'd enjoy doing?" The wind carried her hair away from her face. Even with the guarded expression, she was the prettiest woman he'd ever seen.

"I've seen enough war, enough death. It's an important thing to help soldiers transition home. It might be fulfilling, and something with meaning." He paused, and then said, "I want to stay close to you and Maris, Lindsey."

"Damien, we couldn't even make it through one dinner date. Do you think it's smart to make such a big decision based on our relationship?" She closed her eyes and let out a breath. His heartbeat quickened—was she pushing him away already?

"Let's just call dinner a fluke thing." He hoped to God it was.

"I know you've never wanted a life here, Damien. It's not right to hold you here if it's not what you truly want. The decision has to be yours." He followed her eyes to the white-and-red sailboat that slowly floated along with the white-capped waves.

"This was a dark place for me growing up, but there was one bright light, Lindsey—you." He brushed her hair aside so he could see her face, touched her soft cheek, and guided her eyes to his. "You showed me kindness when no one else would. You sat with me on the bus in grade school, even though my clothes were uncool hand-me-downs from the thrift shop. I stole your lunch and instead of hating me, you brought an extra sandwich every day. You never forgot, not once. Do you have any idea what that meant to me?"

Glistening tears formed in her eyes. She shook her head and gripped his hand. "Why did you push me away then when we were younger?"

"I didn't think I could survive another person I cared for leaving. I want to see what we have here, Lindsey. And I want to give this job a try, not just for that, but because it's something good to balance out all the bad." Was that forgiveness that flittered in her eyes? He scooted a bit closer to her.

"I don't know what's going on between us, but know when I'm with you everything just seems right—better. I want to see what that means, too. Let's both try to be more open. No more secrets, okay?" She leaned her head against his shoulder and he sighed with relief.

"Scout's honor," he whispered into her hair.

"I looked at the contract from the gallery last night," she said after a while. A sandpiper ran by stopping every so often to peck at the sand.

"Lindsey, you don't have to—" She held up her free hand to quiet him.

"It's more than fair. It's unbelievable—I'm not sure someone would really pay that for one canvas, but I'm going to give it a shot. The gallery will take 40 percent of the profits once the pieces start to sell. I did some research and that seems to be a little less than industry standard."

"I believe in you Lindsey, in all of you." He wrapped an arm tightly around her shoulders, afraid that if he loosened his grip she'd slip away from him like sand through open fingers.

DAMIEN RELEASED THE breath he was holding and opened the door to Veterans' Services. A woman with choppy red hair and funky green glasses shot him a smile.

"Mr. Trent?" she asked, and stood up to shake his hand.

"Yes, ma'am. That's me." He returned her smile even though he suddenly wanted to run in the opposite direction.

"Jason will be with you in a few minutes. Please make yourself comfortable." She settled back down at her desk and started clicking away at the computer keys.

He thanked her and chose one of the blue padded chairs. The bubbling fish tank and kids' corner with books and blocks brought a doctor's office to mind. He straightened the deep green tie Lindsey had helped him pick out. The simple shopping trip had turned into a nice afternoon, and gave him renewed hope after their tense dinner date. He had purchased the tie and a simple white collared shirt for his interview. On their way home, they'd stopped at an art shop and Lindsey added some paints and brushes to her basket. While she had been browsing, an elderly man had approached him. *That's a beautiful family you have, son. Cherish it.* To an outsider, it might be easy to mistake them as a family. Caring for Maris seemed to come naturally for him, but doubt still nagged at him like a paper cut. Would it always be this easy, or in time would he change, just like his father had? Or worse, have the urge to run away, like his mother. Part of him still wondered if he was capable of taking on the role of a father at all. And what if things with Lindsey didn't turn out the way he wanted? Would he still be able to see Maris? Damien's stomach clenched. He was scared to death, but he had a real shot with Lindsey this time around. He wouldn't blow it. He wouldn't let shadows of his past chase away the present.

That's why he was sitting in this office building, wearing a tie he desperately wanted to loosen, as sweat beaded on his forehead. He'd handled secret missions in hostile environments. He had kept his head cool and weapon steady when the enemy engaged him, but something about an interview made him want to get up, walk out of the building, and never look back. What made him think he could take a hack at a desk job, when all he'd ever known was the field?

After a short wait, Jay with his happy-go-lucky smile, appeared in the doorway.

"Come on in, Damien." Jay stood in the reception area, tossing a rubber-band ball in one hand. Damien stood and followed Jay out of the waiting room and down a hallway. "I didn't think you'd call, but I'm glad you came in."

"My circumstances changed," Damien said. His throat was as dry as the Sahara Desert.

Jay nodded and turned to his left. "Let's go in here."

The room held one oval conference table with six board-room chairs. He let Jay choose one, then followed his lead and sat across from him. He had to get his cool, or he'd blow the whole damn thing.

"Sorry I wasn't more prompt for our meeting. My sister called to tell me her two-year-old drank some toilet water. She was in a panic. Wanted to know if she should call poison control." His laugh filled the room, and the tight ball in Damien's shoulders eased.

"I got puked on the other day, and thought I was on the set of *The Exorcist.*" Damien grinned. He was surprised that talking about kids was now in his comfort zone.

"Yeah, they really can project at that age. My younger sister's son had colic—it was a nightmare. I don't have any of my own, but man have I taken my fair share of bodily fluids. Was this your friend's baby? The one you mentioned at the bar?"

"Yes, my girlfriend's daughter." His shoulders relaxed at the thought of them. He was sure Lindsey was thinking of him, and would be waiting to hear news of the interview. It was a good feeling, to have someone care for you and cheer you on.

"Ah." Jay gave him a knowing smile. "The reason the circumstances have changed?"

"Yes." He tucked his hands in his lap to keep from fidgeting with his pen. Damn it he was literally sweating bullets. He could shake and water a garden for a month.

"It says a lot about your character, when you take on that responsibility. When you love a child that isn't your own." Jay leaned back casually in the chair, and propped his elbows on the armrests.

Jay had it right. He did love Maris. Damien had come to think of her as his own, and he couldn't picture a future where he wasn't able to watch her grow and laugh and play. Now when he thought of the weeks and years ahead, he always pictured Lindsey and Maris by his side. It made him hopeful, as well as unsettled. How could you feel two such different emotions at once?

They talked for over an hour about his time in the Marines, and his long-term plans. With every joke Jay cracked, the tension unraveled. Soon his hands were out of his pockets, resting against the table, and he no longer had the urge to swipe off his forehead every ten seconds. It didn't feel like an interview at all—just two friends shooting the breeze.

"Damien, I think you'd be a great fit for our case specialist position. You and I would meet with military families to assess their needs, and set them up with available services like housing and job training. It's a salaried position with health benefits, 401(k), and paid vacation." Jay rattled off a salary that seemed fair to Damien.

They sealed the deal with some paperwork and a handshake, and Damien left the office. When the interview had ended, he expected some of the coils of stress lodged between his shoulder blades to ease. This was a big step for him. He never thought he'd try to make a life on the Cape. Now he was locking away a piece of himself that wanted to escape.

He sent Lindsey a quick text with the good news before getting on his bike to head home. That's how he thought of the cottage now, as his home, and Lindsey and Maris were really the only family he had. He was grateful for them, but at times, the responsibility of it and the risk of losing them seemed overwhelming. Would he ever stop fearing he'd be left by the people he cared for?

He walked up the steps to the cottage, carrying his tie in one hand and portfolio in the other. Damien couldn't wait to change out of the stiff shirt. He'd have to get used to this type of wardrobe, as it soon would be his everyday attire. When he swung the door open, Lindsey rushed to him and jumped in his arms. He grinned and pulled her in for a deep kiss, one that made his pulse quicken. When he looked up, he saw the kitchen was filled with red-and-blue balloons.

"Congratulations, Damien! I'm so happy for you." Lindsey's smile was ear-to-ear. "I hope you still like meatloaf and mashed potatoes."

"One of my favorites." He pulled her in for another hug. "You're too good to me, Lindsey."

She stepped back and locked eyes with him. "No, we're good for each other."

Lindsey dived back into the kiss, making his blood heat and ears ring. He hadn't pushed for more, wanting to give her all the time she needed to heal, but now her lips trailed over his neck. Her hot breath against his skin sent shivers down his spine.

She nibbled his earlobe and whispered, "You know, the baby is down for a nap and dinner has another half hour in the oven. I can think of several things we could do in that time."

"I'm up for all of them." He swept her feet off the floor and carried her to the bedroom, closing the door behind them. He laid her down on the bed, and marveled at all that golden hair spread over the white sheets. Once they took this step, there was no going back. The sight of her made his heart thrum. Damien positioned himself beside her, and traced his hand down her face and over her shoulders. Her quick pulse fluttered against his hand when it passed over her neck. It was a wonder that he could make this beautiful woman's heart race, just like his did.

He pulled her tightly against his body, so only clothes

separated them. Her hands roamed under his shirt and over his chest, igniting fires everywhere she touched. She stood up, and undressed slowly in front of him, revealing the glorious curves motherhood had added to her lovely frame. Heat seared through him, and he longed to touch her. She fell into bed with him, pressing that amazing body against his now bare chest. She drove him crazy by placing irresistible kisses over his torso, and tugged at his pants. He struggled to pull them off, wanting her with a need that had taken on a life of its own. Had there ever been a woman so soft and caring, so willing and lovely? When he couldn't stand it any longer he flipped, so he was braced over her.

"Are you sure, Lindsey?" he whispered hoarsely.

"Yes, now Damien," she said arching her hips toward him.

He pressed his lips against her jawline and eased back. "We should use protection."

"You're right. I don't think I'm mentally prepared to lose more sleep with late night feedings."

He chuckled. "Hang on." He opened the nightstand drawer and pulled out a condom. "I bought these a few days ago, you know, just in case."

He entered her slowly, gently, and she gasped with pleasure. When she moved with him, the sweetness of her shot straight through his soul. She owned the key to his heart and unlocked it piece by piece with every sigh and movement. By the time they reached the finish line, he was completely undone by her. It shook him to the core to realize just how much she'd become to him. Damien's life would never be the same now that he'd had her. He would never stop wanting for her, and he'd never stop loving her. She held his heart. She always had, and she always would.

LINDSEY BASKED IN the warmth of Damien's skin against hers. He'd finally taken her to bed and it had been more powerful than any dream or fantasy. He cuddled her close, and every so often pressed a kiss to the top of her head. If only they could stay just like this, tangled up with bodies still warm from loving, for hours, centuries.

She hoped it was the same for him, and doubt trickled in like icy tear drops. Matthew had made it loud and clear that her lack of creativity in bed was one of the reasons he strayed. She silently cursed herself for comparing the two. Damien was nothing like Matthew. Didn't he show her how committed he was to her, every day? If she was always doubting, always second-guessing, the chance to love some-one so completely wonderful might slip past her, like bending to pick up a pretty shell only to have it stolen away by a rolling wave.

"Was it okay for you?" she finally asked. If only her voice didn't hold so many insecurities, so much self-doubt.

"Okay? Lindsey, I don't think there's a word to describe

what that was for me."

She smiled into his chest when he hugged her tighter. Love swamped her heart and it scared her to death. There'd never be another Damien as long as she lived. She had to seize the gift she'd been given, pick up the shell and hold on tight, for a second chance at first love rarely came twice in a lifetime. His hands circled patterns on her back, and goose bumps popped over her arms at his touch.

"Did I hurt you?" His voice was muffled in her hair. The question made her realize Damien had his own uncertainties, too.

"There was no pain. You made sure of it." She snuggled closer and groaned when the oven timer started chirping. She started to stand and Damien pulled her over him. Her hair curtained his face, like a shower of silk. He kissed her deeply and want flamed through her.

"I like burnt meatloaf," he said rolling on top of her. They both laughed.

"And I'd like to end this perfect night without a visit from the fire department." She kissed his forehead, got out of bed, and pulled on some sleep pants. As she padded down the hall to the kitchen, there was an extra spring in her step, and a smile in her heart.

Chapter Twelve

L INDSEY SPENT THE afternoon sorting the letters from Damien's father's house. The dog snored softly beside her and Maris batted at a stuffed whale on her activity mat. Lindsey glanced up at the clock. Damien would be home from work in a few hours, and she'd be able to tell him she was finished. They'd fallen into an easy rhythm that made every day shimmer with possibility.

Lindsey woke with Damien and saw him off to work. Then, she captured the early morning light sparkling over the water with her brushes and paints. When Maris began to stir, she put the project aside and took the baby and Daisy for a long walk on the beach, after they had breakfast. Damien returned home around five, and she made up dinner while he played with the baby. The simplicity of their routine was comforting. Would it always be this way? When she'd started seeing Matthew, everything had been new and fresh, and then things started to change. Small things at first, and before she could blink her eyes, Lindsey was married to a man she didn't know at all. She had to stop comparing her experiences, but Matthew and Damien were the only real relationships she'd ever had.

She picked up the next envelope, and something about the handwriting scratched over the front prickled the hair on her arms. Lindsey tore it open carefully. Her stomach clenched when she scanned the text. She set the letter down, looked out the window for a few moments, and picked it up to reread the note. The note that changed everything for Damien.

Clyde,

I'm sorry for leaving the way I did. You had to know how bad things had gotten between us. I was suffocating. I wanted out and you never listened to a word I said—or maybe you just didn't care. I knew you'd chase after me if I had Damien, but it still stings that you didn't even try to fight for me. I wouldn't be writing you now if I weren't in dire straits. The baby's due in a month. Your baby. I got fired from the diner, the rent needs to be paid, and medical bills are piling up. You owe me for all the grief you've given me, and you owe it to your daughter for being a lousy father before she's even been born. Send cash to the address below.

-Vicky

An address was scribbled below the text. Had Damien's father known his wife was expecting their second child, or had he died thinking he had only a son? Ice coiled in Lindsey's stomach. What kind of mother left her son, and didn't even ask about his well-being? Her heart ached for Damien—the boy and the man. How would he feel when he read his mother's words? When his mother left him, Damien had sealed his heart off. He'd been so deeply hurt that he still felt unworthy of love. He didn't have any other close family members to share the pain with, or to lean against—until now. Somewhere out there Damien had a sister.

When Lindsey heard tires crunching over the driveway through an open window, she glanced back at the clock. How much time had she spent reading the letter over and over again? She nibbled at her lower lip. How would he react when he read the letter? Perhaps she could save him from reading those painful words, while still finding out who his sister was and where she lived. She forced her shoulders to relax. He deserved to know the truth, even if it hurt.

Damien walked through the front door, greeted them, and went to put down his things.

"Is something wrong?" A crease formed between his brows the moment he rounded the corner.

"Damien, come sit down." She patted the couch cushion next to her. If only she could shield him from this.

He arched his eyebrow. "Nothing good has ever come after those words." Damien sat.

"There's something you need to read." She handed him the letter, then tasted blood—she'd chewed her lip raw.

There was a tremor in his hands when he unfolded the sheet of paper. His brows snapped together as he scanned the text. It seemed like an eternity for him to put down the letter and speak.

"She was pregnant when she left. How could she leave us like that?" Damien's body was stiff as a board.

Lindsey squeezed his knee gently trying to comfort. "I didn't want to show you, but that wouldn't have been right. It's from a Boston address. It might be a long shot that your sister still lives there, but I have a friend from college who started her own Boston-based private investigating firm. She's very good from what I've heard. Let me call her, Damien, and we can start searching for her right away. If your mother left when you were about six, your sister would be in her very early twenties—maybe a college student, or just getting out into the workforce."

Damien raised one slash of brow. "Searching for her? I don't want to meet the person my mother chose to love over me. Even if I did, she could be just like my mother—selfish and cold."

"Damien, this is your sister. Your blood relative. How could you move forward with your life, knowing you had a sibling out there?" Lindsey tried to level out her tone. This was his sister. How could he turn his back to her?

"And run the risk of coming face-to-face with my mother again? No thanks." He handed the letter back to her. "You can put it through the shredder, with the other junk."

"Damien, I know this is your choice, but think it through. What if your mother left your sister, just like she did to you, and she's all alone without any family? You didn't have a mother growing up, but she didn't have a father. You each got half. Maybe she'd be able to offer you some closure."

Damien swiped his hands over his face. His jaw was set in a hard line. "I've thought it through, Lindsey, and the answer is no. I don't want to find her. I don't want to know who she is. Just leave it alone." Damien was standing now. The grief and angst rolled off him like a tidal wave. She couldn't leave it alone. How could she make him understand that his sister might be the missing puzzle piece to help him click his past into place?

"What if she's sweet and kind? Someone you'd grow to love? Damien, you could have a wonderful family member out there, and you're brushing her aside. What if she needs you, too?" Lindsey stood up and faced him head-on.

"Your outlook is much different than mine, Lindsey, because you had a perfect childhood with parents who loved you unconditionally. It was all sunshine and rainbows for you. Not me. I know what she could be like. I can't handle the disappointment."

His words stung—that had been his intent.

Maris started to cry and Lindsey quickly picked her up off the floor.

"I need to get some air." Damien angled his body toward the front door and looked back at her. "Don't wait up." He grabbed his wallet off the table and walked out of the house.

For the second time in their relationship, she was completely unsure of their future. Lindsey cuddled Maris closer. Her family meant so much to her. She wanted Damien to experience that, too, but he'd made it perfectly clear that he was vehemently against it. A light bulb went off. Perhaps she could find his sister, determine where she was, and what she was like. If she seemed like a good person, she could admit what she'd done and introduce them, and if not, Damien would never know the difference.

She thought back to the painting he'd sold behind her back. At the time, she'd been crushed that he didn't consider her feelings, but now she understood he was just trying to give her something she so desperately wanted but was afraid to grasp for herself. If she did this, wouldn't it be exactly like how he'd molded a bit of her future without her consent? Of course, there were multiple people involved in Damien's situation whose lives might be impacted if she took action.

Damien had such an awful childhood, one that had scarred his soul. If only he could develop a relationship with his little sister, maybe it could heal some of the hurt his parents had inflicted on him. Maybe, he wouldn't feel so alone anymore. Her conscience played a game of tug-of-war. The last thing she wanted to do was betray his trust. It was really a decision he needed to make on his own, but she wanted to help him heal, to be whole. Sometimes, the best families were the ones you made on your own, but somewhere, Damien had a sister, too. One phone call could change everything, but what if it wasn't for the best?

As the baby napped, Lindsey walked through the cottage picking up toys, and rearranging this and that. The only sound in the house was the faint creak of floorboards under her feet and the whirl of the overhead kitchen fan. Why did she have to read that letter? It nagged at her. Did his sister have a terrible upbringing, too? Was she struggling? Lindsey had a gut feeling, one that was telling her to pick up the phone.

ONCE MARIS WOKE up, Lindsey wrapped her in a light blanket, took her phone off the kitchen table, and stepped out onto the deck. She scrolled through her contacts and picked out Alexandra Macintyre's number.

She drew in the salty air when she heard the ring tone. If only she knew what was the right thing to do for Damien.

The other line clicked, and a familiar voice sounded.

"Macintyre Investigating." Her friend's tone was brisk and to the point.

"Alex, it's Lindsey." Alex had been a law student and Lindsey's roommate during senior year of college. They'd lost touch after Lindsey had married Matthew and Alex had started her own firm.

"What a nice voice to hear on a crappy day. How the hell are you?"

"Divorced, with a new baby, and a boyfriend you'd definitely approve of." Lindsey smiled into the phone. "And you?"

"Perpetually single, working sixteen-hour days, couldn't be happier. Glad you left that scumbag. He had a look about him. And a new baby? Congratulations!"

"He was sleeping with his secretary." Lindsey could look at it objectively now, without the sting of rejection.

"His loss," Alex said simply. Lindsey could imagine her shrugging her shoulders, with her feet propped up on her desk. Lindsey heard a bark on the other line.

"You got a dog!" Her friend had always wanted one.

"That's Hank, my partner in crime, and the only guy in my life. Wait till you meet him. Daisy will look like a little mushroom next to him."

Lindsey laughed.

"So, this friend of mine, his name is Damien, found out he might have a long-lost sister. The problem is, he doesn't want to find her."

"And you do, because you're always trying to make things better for people, even if they don't want the help. That's like swimming in shark-infested waters, Lindsey."

"I know it." She sighed.

"Okay, as long as you do. Email me what you have. I'll let you know what I dig up," Alex said.

"I will and charge me for your time."

"That's insulting, Lindsey. Just send the email."

She hung up the phone, and looked out at the sea. Her friend always found what she was looking for. Alex had an uncanny knack for solving riddles and finding what was lost. When Damien found out, would he forgive her instead of walking away? She was taking a big risk doing this, but she had to try for Damien.

Maris squirmed in her arms and she bounced the baby gently on her knee. Lindsey chuckled when Maris's eyes crossed, as she tried to look down at a bubble of drool. She wanted Damien to experience the love of family so desperately, to have a special bond with the sibling he'd never known. The wind had picked up, and dark clouds started rolling over the horizon. When the first bolt of lightning zigzagged over the ocean, she took Maris inside. She tried to call Damien to make sure he was okay, but the call went right to voicemail. Her heart weighed heavily in her chest and her throat was so tight, it hurt to swallow. Would Damien, who'd been wonderful for so long, end up like his mother and walk out on them, too? Was she an idiot to put faith in him? Maybe her own wishful thinking was making him out to be something he wasn't.

She had to brace herself for the realization that things wouldn't always be easy with Damien. Self-preservation had her tucking away her phone, a physical action to help her disconnect from him. Maris was her life now. She wouldn't count on another to make her life and her baby's a happy one. That was up to her. Lindsey locked the sliding glass door and took some colorful picture books from the coffee table. Even before Maris was born, she loved reading her the short tales. Her daughter's gaze traveled over the bright images as she read Eric Carle's tale about *The Very Hungry Caterpillar*. It didn't matter how much she hurt, so long as Maris never experienced the pain of an adult she loved closing the door on their relationship—something Matthew had already done. Damien would have to decide what type of role he wanted in their lives, and she'd have to determine if trying was worth the potential heartache.

Lindsey's skin tingled when her phone vibrated inside her jean's pocket. Her shoulders loosened. It had to be Damien letting her know where he was and that he was safe. She glanced down and didn't recognize the number. More likely Alex, calling from another office line or a new cell phone.

With a quick swipe of her thumb, she picked up the call.

"Hello?" Lindsey opened *Brown Bear, Brown Bear, What Do You See?* to keep Maris occupied.

"Lindsey, we need to talk." She shut her eyes. Damn. Her ex-husband's voice was like razor wire.

"Matthew, I've signed the papers, you've started fresh, what's left to discuss?" She hated the breathless notes that peppered her speech. How could the sound of his voice, thousands of miles away, make ice snake down her back?

"I've been thinking about the baby."

Everything froze inside her. Lindsey didn't want Matthew involved. A selfish piece of her didn't want to share Maris. She was the one who woke every two hours in the night, who went through the extraordinary pain of labor, who poured every piece of herself into loving Maris. The son of a bitch on the other end of the call had to use the word "baby," because he had no clue if Maris was a boy or a girl. He didn't even know her name. Her words were locked in her throat.

"Lindsey, I want to see my kid. Do I need to call my lawyer?" Of course, he would threaten, before she even had a chance to speak. His lawyer had played dirty, used every loophole, and rendered Lindsey with nothing.

"Matthew, you haven't supported this baby in any way. Not one. Why do you want to see her now?"

"A girl, then. I would have preferred a son. Regardless, it's my right to see her." Arrogance flowed through his tone. "I'll be visiting next week. Give me the address, so I can put it in my GPS."

Lindsey gritted her teeth. "Will Florence be coming?" Matthew was silent for a moment, giving her great satisfaction.

"Florence discovered she can't have children. I couldn't be with someone so…flawed."

She could hear the disgust in his voice, and would have felt sorry for the pretty assistant, if she hadn't knowingly slept with a married man—her husband. So, there was her answer. Matthew needed to see for himself the baby he'd produced, to eliminate any insecurities about his ability to father a child. He didn't care about Maris. The tips of her ears burned. If she looked in a mirror, they'd be bright red, and her face flushed with anger.

"I'm sure she didn't want to be with someone so perfect anyways." Lindsey couldn't control her sarcasm or her temper for another minute. Why bother trying to be cordial?

"I see you've developed an attitude. Check it when I vis-it."

"Get off your high horse, Matthew. Things have changed. I'm not the same meek woman you left."

She heard him sneer, then snicker. "Maybe I should bring along the lawyer, to remind you how powerful I am. I could take that baby, have full parental rights, before you could wipe that blank stare off your face."

Her breath caught in her throat and blood roared in her ears. "Why would you do that? You know nothing about raising a child. Not one single thing! You've never even seen her before!"

"To prove I could. And I said nothing of raising her. That's an au pair's job. My work is too important to putt around with a baby all day."

He couldn't legally take the baby unless he could prove her to be a negligent parent—which she wasn't. Still, her thready pulse and the ice that spread in a wave from her face all the way down to the tips of her toes, told her she'd have a panic attack if she didn't end this call now. She rattled off the address, and hung up. Lindsey hunched over and hugged Maris close. He couldn't take her, could he? Lindsey's heart fluttered quickly in her chest. No, he couldn't, but all the logical thinking in the world wasn't going to calm her racing pulse. He had strong and corrupt lawyers that could make things very difficult for her if that's what Matthew wanted.

What right did he have to threaten her like that? Their whole marriage had been about leveraging control. She should have left him sooner, but he wore her down until she doubted everything she did or said. Lindsey was just regaining her confidence, only to be slapped down again. Maris was her entire world and he wouldn't use her love for their child against her. Lindsey had to grow a set, and stand firm.

The truth was, his words had left her shaken. More so than she'd like to admit. She'd always wanted to be a mother, to have a happy, normal family. She was so close to that now with Maris. She couldn't lose her baby. Why did he have to pop up, today of all days, when she was already mentally exhausted from her showdown with Damien? She hated to think the words, because nothing was ever guaranteed, but it wasn't fair. It wasn't fair that her ex could pop out of nowhere and threaten to exercise his parental rights. It wasn't fair that she scraped by while he didn't contribute an ounce to raising their child, and it wasn't fair that Damien, the man who she should be able to lean on when she needed it, had flown the coop because it was easier to run from his problems than to face them. When she was done with her personal pity powwow, Lindsey took a deep breath. In through her nose, out through her mouth, just like the therapist she'd visited after the divorce had taught her.

No one was going to take Maris from her. That was the way Matthew worked. Threaten, gain control of the situation, and get what he wanted. Lindsey needed to man up. She wasn't just acting for herself now, she was fighting for her baby's rights, too. Maris couldn't talk yet, or tell her lousy father how she felt or what she wanted, so Lindsey would be her voice and when the time came, she'd make sure it was strong, clear, and unafraid.

Chapter Thirteen

DAMIEN WAS REELING from the news. He had a sister. Not a half sister or a stepsister—a full sibling. He absently pressed a fist to his chest to ease the ache in his heart. It wasn't physical pain, but a deep disturbance that had rocked him off his feet. Maybe it was the realization that his mother not only left him, but kept him away from his sister, as well. What made his sister so important that she chose to keep that child instead of Damien?

He hadn't handled the news well. Perhaps he wasn't that different from his old man after all. He'd raised his voice at Lindsey, frightened Maris to tears, and fled to the bar. He sat alone, brooding over Lindsey's words. Of course, he was curious about his sister, but he wasn't sure if the risks outweighed the reward. Could he handle the disappointment of meeting her, only to find she was just like his mother? It was better to leave things alone. He needed to focus on the new life he was building rather than mess with the past. Damien wouldn't always be able to outrun it, but he could try to accept what was and move forward.

He rested his elbows against the worn pine bar top and

rubbed his hands over his face. For the second time in a matter of weeks, he'd hurt Lindsey. Maybe he wasn't cut out for a relationship after all. She was a good woman, and she deserved better than what he had to offer. At the moment, being a hermit who lived alone on a mountaintop seemed like a good option. Somewhere he couldn't hurt anyone.

"Is it a bad sign that I'm running into you at another bar?" Jay stood next to him, grinning.

Damien didn't want to deal with Jay's sunny outlook when a personal black cloud was brewing over him. He lifted his bottle, took a long sip, and set it down.

"Might be for both of us." He angled his head toward Jay.

"You don't look like you want company," Jay said. He settled on the barstool next to Damien anyway. "But that's usually when someone needs a shoulder the most."

Did he ever get upset? Mad at the cards he'd been dealt? Damien's eyes wandered to Jay's scarred face as he ordered a cola. He took a breath and closed his eyes for a moment. Jay had been through just as much as him. Damien was just lucky his scars were hidden under a shirt and in his heart.

Jay swiveled the stool toward Damien. "So, what brings you to this dive when you have a woman waiting at home?" Jay leaned back in the chair and crossed his arms loosely over his chest.

"She found something in my father's junk. It complicates things." He released a ragged breath and looked down at his beer.

"Ah. So, you killed the messenger." Jay gave him an understanding nod and leaned forward to rest his elbows against the bar top.

"Yeah, I guess you could say that. My father would have done the same. Explode at my mother, run off to the bar to get loaded, only to be hauled back to the house by the police."

"From where I'm sitting, it looks like you're nursing a beer and thinking things through. Solitude can help us sort things out, you know. You sure don't look like you're going to get hauled away by the cops anytime soon." Jay took a sip of his soda, and watched a pitcher step up to the mound on the ancient TV behind the bar.

Damien looked down at his solitary beer. His father would have been a six-pack deep by now, drinking to wipe away the day. Jay was right. Damien had needed a spot to clear his head. Maybe he needed to stop being so hard on himself. He spent so much time trying to push away any trace of his parents, he didn't know who he really was. How could he start an important relationship or care for a child, when he wasn't even sure of himself?

"What about you?" he asked, and Jay's brown eyes broke from the TV to meet Damien's. "Got a woman waiting at home?"

"If I did, I sure as hell wouldn't be here." A lone dimple popped in his cheek. "This isn't a face made for romance."

He gestured to the right side of his head.

"You're not looking at the right girls, then." Jay's face was a stamp of courage and a reminder of the price of war.

"Maybe you're right, but for now work keeps me busy enough. Maybe the right one will come along someday." Jay drained his soda and set down the empty glass.

Damien hoped one did. He'd only known Jay a short time, but he was a good person, one who would put everything into a relationship. It made him think of his own, and how he should get going so he could put things straight. Two elderly red-faced men got up from the bar and walked to the exit laughing heartily at something.

"Jay, you have sisters. What's it like having siblings?" Damien drained the last of his beer and signaled to the bartender for another.

"Just about the best thing in the world. We've always been close. My parents live in town, too. It's nice to have a support net, you know?" Jay said. A waiter whizzed by with a towering plate of cheesy nachos. The buzz of chattering patrons and the blurred undertones of the TV echoed around him.

"I don't, really. My mom left when I was young. Dad didn't hang around much." For the second time in his life, Damien had told someone about his family dynamic. Was he going soft, or did he just need someone else to lean on? "Lindsey, she found a letter from my mom that said I have a sister out there." Damien stared at the wall in front of him.

"And you're not sure if you want to make contact because it could change things—maybe for the worst?" Jay's eyes held compassion and it poured out to Damien, reaching the pit of his heart. He'd found family in Lindsey and Maris, and now he'd found a friend in Jay. Shouldn't he just be grateful for the good people he had around him, instead of trying to shoe-horn one more into his life?

"That's exactly it. And if I were to reach out, it would open up the possibility of contact from my mother. I'm not sure if I'll ever be ready to face her." Damien propped his elbows on the counter and looked at Jay.

"I get that. She left you, and you don't owe her a damn thing. If you don't think you'll regret not reaching out to your sister, then don't. But think on this. She might need to meet you a whole lot more than you do her." Jay slapped him on the shoulder, squeezed. "Nothing's ever easy, is it?"

Damien laughed. "Nope. Doesn't seem that way." Glass clinked against wood as the bartender set another frosty bottle in front of him. They watched the TV and relaxed for a few minutes in silence.

"And how about Lindsey? Will she let it go, or will she keep pushing you to find your sister?" Jay asked.

"I guess I'll find out. She only wants what's best for me—I know that. I should go apologize before I have to sleep under the stars." Damien pulled out his wallet, and tossed some bills on the table.

"It's a shame we're wired to lash out at the ones we love

most," Jay said.

Damien wondered if he was that transparent. The warmth and attraction he'd held in his heart for Lindsey fueled him to help when her car had broken down. A smile brushed his lips when he thought of her hugely pregnant belly. It made it really hard to leave Chatham when his heart started to be dragged toward love, like a toy sailboat being sucked into a swirling funnel of water. He was constantly faced with a hard question that he had to reach deep down to answer. Damien wasn't really ready to go there, afraid of what the response might be. What was best for Lindsey and Maris? He could stay, and things might be just grand, but what if eventually he changed like his father had? He didn't want to be the root of someone else's pain—especially the two people he cared for most.

"Let me drive you home, brother. I haven't even had a drink yet." Jay's voice broke his thoughts.

He was fine to drive, but better safe than sorry. "All right. Let's hit the road. I have groveling to do."

Jay's full-bodied laugh inspired a sense of comradery and friendship he hadn't experienced since Johnny. Someday, he'd tell Jay about him. It was rare he actually wanted to open up to someone else, but lately there were a whole lot of feelings fighting for space in his heart—he just didn't know what to let stick, or if the choice was out of his hands completely. The same heart he often thought of as two sizes too small, like his favorite Christmas tale, seemed to be growing three sizes a day. If the people he'd accepted into his life decided to leave, he'd be crushed with the velocity of an ant being hit by a transport truck.

They left the bar and got into Jay's Jeep. Damien rattled off directions, then enjoyed the slap of salty sea-air against his skin as they drove, top down, toward the cottage.

"You know, you should come for dinner some night. Lindsey would love you and she makes a hell of a meatloaf."

Jay glanced at him through the dark and Damien saw a shadow of a smile. For a moment, it was as if he was driving with the ghost of Johnny. When the temperature had dropped, and they rolled out their sleeping bags in the sand, Johnny would always smile through the dark, talking about the Big Mac he was going to have the second he touched U.S. soil.

"Offer accepted," Jay said.

They pulled up to the cottage and Damien thanked Jay for the ride. The headlights of the Jeep flashed away, once he was inside. Lindsey was sitting at the kitchen table with a cup of tea.

Damien hesitated. "I bumped into Jay, and he gave me a ride home." He tucked his hands into his pockets and stood in the center of the kitchen. Fear squeezed at his heart when Lindsey just looked down into her steaming mug.

"Do you ever feel like we're on the cusp of something really great, and then the past sneaks up to bite us in the ass?" she said.

He was aware of his heart thumping in his chest, as he looked at Lindsey, slumped over the table with defeat written across her face. He pulled a chair beside her and sat down.

"Linds, I'm still figuring myself out. The news was a bombshell to me. I needed air. I need to think it out. And there I go with the 'I' and 'me.' I'm still learning how to live with someone I care about, and I realize that means thinking of the 'we' and 'us,' before I run off with my tail tucked between my legs." He stroked a hand down her soft hair.

"I got my own bombshell after you left." Her voice was flat and tired. The squeeze that clutched his heart clamped.

"What is it, Lindsey? Are you okay, your parents?" She was silent for one breath, then two. The howl of wind and the rushing surf made a dramatic symphony from the open porch screen.

"Matthew wants to see Maris." She looked up at him and her eyes shimmered with tears.

"Well, shit. After all this time?" Inside Damien's head screamed. Her ex was coming back to see the baby and there could only be one reason for it. To win back Lindsey. He'd manipulated and convinced her to do things before. What if he persuaded her to move home? Or worse, what if Lindsey decided that because Maris was his child, they should be a family?

"He wasn't here. Not for any of it. I cried myself to sleep night after night when I first left him. How would I raise the baby on my own? How would I get through the pain of labor without him by my side? Now I can't stand the thought of seeing him, or of watching him hold the daughter that's of his blood, but not of his heart." She pinched the bridge of her nose. "Why do things always have to be so complicated? Why can't we just...be?"

He wrapped his arms around her and held onto her tight, as if she might slip through his fingers at any moment. It wasn't only him who had demons, it was her, too. How could they make a future together when they kept getting sucked into their past problems? He breathed in her beachy scent mingled with tears. Matthew had hurt her, but as of lately, he had, too. Maybe neither of them deserved her at all.

Chapter Fourteen

L INDSEY HAD SO much on her mind that it was like
middle school band lessons were in session inside her
head. The sounds of the brass, woodwind, and percussions
were thrumming so loudly she could barely think. Of course,
it wasn't instruments that clogged her brain and left her
mind limp like one of Daisy's stuffed chew toys. Her relationship with Damien held so many unknowns, and now she
was second-guessing her decision to ask Alex for intel on
Damien's long-lost sister.

Lindsey had fallen for Damien hard and fast. Her heart,
mind, and soul were on the line. She knew there was a real
chance of losing him once he discovered what she'd done,
but she wanted him to be happy, and to her that meant
finding his sister at all costs. She supposed locating his sister
wouldn't guarantee that Damien would be happy at all.
She'd always equated happiness with having a solid, loving
family. What if for Damien, family were the people you
chose and not those with the same DNA? Maybe their
definitions of family were different, and if so, did she really
only screw things up?

She sighed and looked at the mountain of dishes in the kitchen sink, piling up like Mount Vesuvius. Lindsey composed herself, picked up a dish, and started scrubbing. When she received commission from her first painting, a dishwasher would be the first thing she checked off her to-do list.

When she had shared his mother's letter the week before, a steel wall surfaced around Damien. That moment had brought hard questions to the surface. If Damien couldn't rationally discuss feelings of his past with her, how could they handle bigger problems that arose in their relationship later on? Every time the going got tough, would he slam that steel wall shut and leave her on the outside looking in?

She'd had enough secrets and lies when she'd been with Matthew, and by God she was done being someone's doormat. Done.

Matthew's call had shaken her to the core. She wished she told him he couldn't visit, but his manipulative words had frightened her. Matthew had insisted on coming, and he was the father after all. Everything was such a mess, and her relationship with Damien was volatile. Maybe, Lindsey was just meant to be single. She didn't feel strong enough to fight off Matthew, and then walk on eggshells with Damien. She wanted them to be an honest and open couple, and they were, so long as they treaded lightly around Damien's past or anything to do with it. Was she being too hard on him? She knew Damien had faced significant trauma. Maybe she was the problem. Was she so set on finding this perfect, happy relationship that she was trying to fit a triangle block into a circle hole?

Perhaps her upbringing with two great parents, albeit a little overbearing and sometimes judgmental, really did color her world in a different light. If Damien was just trying to preserve himself from the pain of his past, who was she to tear away the barrier between the last connection he had? Life was so darn complicated sometimes.

She let out a long sigh. Lindsey and Damien would have to have a heart-to-heart, but right now, Matthew was her biggest worry. Lindsey snickered at the thought of Matthew's perfectly manicured hands getting soiled while changing a diaper. She secretly hoped Maris would throw up all over one of his neatly pressed shirts. Still, she had to let him come. What choice did she have? Maris was his, too, by blood. It tore deeply into the core of her heart, because Matthew was no father to her at all. He didn't care for her, and he didn't love her. Someday, she'd have to explain to Maris why her biological father wasn't there for her. She absently massaged her temples to ease the ache there.

Lindsey jerked, and the plate she was holding clattered to the ground. It shattered in a thousand pieces as her cell phone shrilled wildly on the counter beside her. Lindsey released the breath she'd been holding when she saw Alex's name flash across the screen. Taking the baby monitor with her, she pulled the slider open and stepped on the deck. The warm air didn't hold any comfort today, and she angled her body away from the gusts of wind as they snapped wisps of hair against her face.

Alex's no-nonsense voice greeted her, then softened. The knot building inside her stomach could easily trump the world's largest ball of yarn.

"Linds, I found her," Alex said. "Her name is Kate."

"Well, what do you think?" Lindsey asked, desperate for input or any inkling that she'd done the right thing. "Her character—is she someone Damien would want to meet?"

"Listen, I'm doing some work outside Boston today, for a corporation in Carver. Just wrapping up now, actually. I can be there in, say, an hour or so? We can go over the details in person, and then you can decide."

Lindsey's plate was pretty full with Damien's new boss coming for dinner, a baby to tend to, and a house to clean, but learning about Damien's sister was high up on her priority list.

"Can you stay for dinner?" Lindsey wrapped her free hand around her stomach, which was churning with angst.

"And not eat one of the frozen disks in my apartment freezer? Yes, please." Alex laughed and a ghost of a smile formed on Lindsey's face.

"Perfect. Just a heads-up, Damien will be bringing a friend home from the office."

"Nothing would stand between me and a home-cooked meal."

"Or any meal." Lindsey laughed now, too, as she remembered her friend's intense love of the cafeteria food in college.

"Hey, a girl has to eat," Alex said before clicking off the line. Lindsey had always been semi-jealous of Alex's lithe frame. The ability to down fast-food like it was a part-time job and never gain an ounce was Alex's super power. Lindsey quickly learned that Alex woke before the sun, slipped on her running shoes, snuck out of the dormitory, and pounded the pavement while the rest of the world slept.

The static on the monitor picked up, and she looked at the screen. Maris was stirring. She had about ten minutes to finish up the dishes and spin through the house for a quick sweep of the floors. She blew out a breath and got to work. As she dried dishes and tucked them into the cabinet, her mind whirled with possibilities of Damien's sister—who she was, what she did, how she looked. Anything to keep her mind off the giant ball of yarn as it spun wickedly in her belly. God, she hoped she'd done the right thing for Damien.

In the end, Maris gave her an extra half hour to do housework, and Lindsey was quite pleased with her accomplishments. The house was spotless, and a shepherd's pie was assembled and ready to be popped in the oven. A car door slammed outside, and she stood up with Maris, who was cuddled in her arms. Lindsey glanced out the window just in time to see Alex's long legs slide out from the black SUV. As she walked to the house, the sea breeze tossed her fiery hair, swiping the choppy strands against her chin. She wore dark jeans, a black T-shirt, and simple sneakers. Nothing about her friend had changed.

When Alex got close enough, she swung an arm around Lindsey, and peered down at Maris who looked back with wide eyes.

"Can you believe we were ever that tiny?" Alex whispered. A hint of unfamiliar awe swam through the currents of her voice.

"When she was first born, she seemed so small and so fragile. I carried her like she was made of eggshells." Lindsey grinned at Alex.

"I won't be holding her." Her friend smiled, eyes still locked on the baby. "There's way too much responsibility wrapped in that bundle of blanket."

"I won't force you." Lindsey glanced down to the leather portfolio in Alex's hands.

"I can see you're chomping at the bit. Let's go inside and we can look these over. Great place, by the way." With one fluid movement, she opened the door to the cottage and breezed in. She stopped in the center of the kitchen, sniffed the air like a basset hound, and let out a long sigh. "Please tell me that smell is dinner."

"It is. Shepherd's pie. I was trying to think of something manly to make with Jay coming over. That's the best I could come up with."

"That's pretty darn impressive. If I had a child, plus had to take care of a house, there wouldn't be enough freezer storage in the world for all the Stouffer's frozen dinners I'd need to buy." Alex plopped down at the kitchen table, and Lindsey pulled over Maris's activity chair so she could bat at the flowers and owls that hung above the arched pink canopy. Once she settled Maris in and buckled her securely, she switched her focus to Alex, and the single manila file that she produced from the case.

Lindsey pressed her hand to her chest, and the wild flap of her heart thrummed against her hand. "Oh, my gosh. I didn't think I'd be this nervous," she admitted.

Alex eyed her squarely from across the table. "Linds, you can change your mind. No one would know any different. This guy you're seeing—Damien—how will he take it?"

Lindsey shook her head. "I'm not sure. Deep down, I think he's always envied those who have a family and craved one of his own. Now he has that chance."

"You can't always count on blood. Sometimes the happy family we all seek is the furthest thing from our God-given relatives." Alex cracked the file ever so slightly. "If you're sure?"

"Yes, I'm sure. Damien needs to know. He'll never be able to move forward with his life if he can't face his past." Alex opened the file on the wooden table and Lindsey forced herself to breath normally.

"She's squeaky clean, Lindsey. No records, no traffic violations, no suspensions from school." Alex slid a stack of photos over to Lindsey. On the glossy paper, she saw Damien's sister, blissfully unaware that her picture was being snapped by a stranger. She cringed at the invasion of privacy. There were images of Kate walking across campus in relaxed jeans, a college T-shirt, and a stuffed backpack. Ones of her studying on the green with her brows furrowed in concentration. There was no denying this was Damien's sister. Her glossy hair, black as ink, fell just above her shoulders, and the eyes, that coastal-blue, was reflected on the photos. Unlike her brother, her build looked very petite.

"She's beautiful." Lindsey's voice, barely a whisper, cracked as she shifted through the photos again.

"And smart. Her GPA is a 3.9 and she's going for a dual degree in psychology and early childhood education. She works part-time at a twenty-four-hour diner. Seems to burn the candle at both ends. There's something driving her focus, and I think it's the mother."

Lindsey's brows snapped together. "Damien's mother is in Boston?"

Alex frowned, and Lindsey's heart sank like quicksand.

"Was, Lindsey," Alex said. "She died at New Horizons, a treatment center for addiction. She overdosed. From what I can tell, Kate was footing the bills to keep her there. It looks like Kate may have been born during detox. Baby and mom had a two-month stint at the hospital in a special rehabilitation center. I didn't include information on his mother's passing in the file. He shouldn't learn that news from a piece of paper."

Tears welled in the corners of Lindsey's eyes, blurring the papers and the room in front of her. Had she just popped the lid off Pandora's box? Damien had just lost his father, and now she had discovered his mother had passed, too. She pressed her hand to her temple. Lindsey didn't want to think of what this poor girl had gone through. It said something about her spirit that she forged on, going to college and holding a job, even though life kept knocking her back. Damien and his sister were tough as steel, and maybe the upbringing they shared would help weld them together.

"Are you going to tell him?" Alex asked, when Lindsey checked on the casserole inside the oven.

"They need each other. I'll tell him when the time's right," Lindsey said. Would there ever be a right time to tell Damien she'd snuck around behind his back? Like an old reel of film, the scene of how she'd break the news to Damien kept streaming through her mind. Each one ended with his back turned to her. Ended with everything they'd built crumbling like a house of ash.

"You can keep the file," Alex said. "But I'd tuck it away, because there're two seriously hot men walking down the drive."

Lindsey peeked out the front window and her eyes went straight to Damien. The cuffs of his crisp white dress shirt were rolled up at the elbows, leaving his strong, tan forearms bare. The same arms that held her at night. The ones that made her feel safe and wanted. His lips curved into a smile at something Jay had said. It softened all the hard angles and planes of his face.

Damien looked up and caught her eye. He grinned and waved. The two men stomped up on the porch, bringing a trail of sand with them, while jesting causally like old friends.

"Lindsey," Jay said and pulled her into an easy half hug. "It's nice to finally meet the person I hear about for the better part of the day." His warm eyes crinkled at the corners, genuine and sincere. Damien had told her about his face, but the scars pained her all the same. Lindsey introduced Alex to the men. It was interesting that Alex's hand rested in Jay's for more than a casual moment. Throughout the meal she noticed Alex's eyes wandering over Jay's face. She knew her friend well enough to know it wasn't the burns she kept glancing at. Jay looked up every so often, and shot her a lazy smile.

When it was time for Maris's feeding, Lindsey retreated into the nursery. She was surprised when Damien snuck in and shut the door behind them.

"Can you believe the looks flying between them? I'll bet you anything that I won't be the one taking Jay home tonight."

Lindsey's lips curved smugly. "I don't make a bet I know I'm going to lose. Alex's intentions are written all over her face. She's not exactly the bashful type."

"Jay's eating it up. He doesn't get much female attention. This is really good for his ego." He clasped Lindsey's chin and brushed his lips against hers. "I hope you didn't miss the looks I was sending you."

"How could I? They were enough to add an extra layer of singe to the shepherd's pie." She had tried not to worry about overcooking dinner. It was one of those things that would have set Matthew off like a cannon.

"It was delicious, and I don't think either of our guests will be complaining about their dining experience tonight." He kissed her forehead. It was a sentimental gesture she'd never get sick of. What was it about a kiss on the forehead that made a lovely warmth spread through her chest? He stroked a few strands of stray hair away from her face, and that warmth swirled down to the tips of her feet. Damien gave her those little toe-curling moments every woman dreamed of. Except he wasn't a dream at all. He was real and solid. She pushed away any thought of the file and of his sister. Once their friends left, tonight was going to be just about them. At least in bed, she could show him how she felt, without having to put her overwhelming emotions into words.

As predicted, the evening ended with Alex offering to drive Jay home. As Damien and Lindsey waved goodbye, they shared a victory high-five behind their backs. With Maris swaddled and tucked into her crib, Lindsey slid into the bedroom and settled under the covers next to Damien.

"How are you feeling about tomorrow?" Damien asked.

The last thing Lindsey wanted to think about right now was her ex coming to see their child for the first time.

"I'm trying not to feel anything about it." She snuggled closer and let her cheek rest on his bare chest. The steady thrum of his heart echoed against her cheek.

Damien leaned back to glance down at her, and frowned. "Do you still have feelings for him, Lindsey?"

"That's not what I meant. I'm trying to put aside my anger toward him. I don't want Maris to sense any hostility from me. He's her father after all, even though he hasn't been here. I haven't seen him in over a year."

Damien nodded and pulled her back against him. "I'm not budging. You know that, right?" His hands ran through the length of her hair, then back again. "If you want privacy, I'll give it, but while he's here, so am I."

She knew it shouldn't give her pleasure, but the fierce protectiveness in his voice sent a thrill straight through her. He was so resilient and so completely male. Anticipation flooded her when he cupped the back of her neck. He brushed kisses over each eyelid, and one on the tip of her nose, before parting her lips with his. She sank into his skin, drank in his scent, and overflowed with desire for him. They made love with an intensity that matched the heightened emotions of the day ahead. She knew it wouldn't be simple to come face-to-face with Matthew, and Damien was showing her in every delicious way she could imagine that she belonged to him.

Chapter Fifteen

MARIS WAILED AND Damien crossed his arms tightly against his chest. The prick was holding her all wrong. He wanted to bat the city slicker's hands away from the baby, and boot him out on his ass. Hard enough that those salmon-colored shorts filled with sand, and maybe a pinching crab or two. Matthew had walked into the cottage with a chip on his shoulder, examining the house with an upturned nose. It took all Damien's military restraint to hold back when Matthew kept making belittling snipes.

Matthew cleared his throat. "This might be a nice weekend getaway for two, if you like a more…rustic style, but it's hardly a conducive place to raise my child." Was this guy serious? What a pompous ass. Damien was about to jump in, but Lindsey got there first. Her nostrils flared, and a red flush spread over her cheeks.

Lindsey's eyes narrowed. "In what way?"

Matthew shifted his body toward Lindsey, blocking Damien out of the conversation.

"Well, do you remember how our perfectly manicured Colonial had two stories with the master suite on the first floor, and the bedrooms on the second? You could get a decent night's sleep if the baby was upstairs and you couldn't hear all its screeching. Then you wouldn't have those dark circles under your eyes."

Damien's throat was dry. It choked him like a tie that was far too tight, and added to his irritation. "What you're talking about is neglect," he said in a low voice. How many times had he cried himself to sleep as a kid, wishing his father would come up and hug him instead of hitting him? To tell him everything would be okay without his mother.

"If Maris cries, it's because she needs something. She might be hungry or uncomfortable. Like she is now, because you're holding her like she's a ticking time bomb that's going to ruin your shirt." Damien got up from the loveseat and took Maris out of his hands.

Her crying instantly stopped. His baby was a good judge of character. Except she wasn't really his baby, even though he wished she was. She was so tiny and vulnerable, it made him want to protect her in a way that he wasn't as a child. He loved her thick mop of hair that was softer than the feathers from a down comforter. Maris had started smiling, too, and man, did those little grins melt his heart.

Maris and Lindsey made him want to stay in the one place he'd always wanted to run from. He didn't like being obligated to care for others, because the people who should have raised him did a piss-poor job of it. He didn't want to follow in his parents' footsteps, so he hadn't wanted a family of his own, but they made him want things he'd never wanted—ever. The vagabond lifestyle he imagined suddenly seemed very empty, and a quiet life shared with two special people seemed like heaven. In his arms, the baby snuggled closer to his shirt and her eyelids dipped. It was right around nap time.

"She's getting sleepy," Lindsey said. "I'm going to put her down for a nap, then you can tell us why you came here in the first place, Matthew." Lindsey moved toward Damien and gently gathered Maris in her arms. She was a good mother. The kind every child deserved.

With Lindsey out of the room, they both sat in stony silence. There was no question why Matthew was here. Things had gotten stale with the secretary and he was here to take Lindsey back. Meeting Matthew gave him a glimpse of the life she might've had before she moved back to the Cape. The guy was all pomp. He'd looked up the address they'd once shared, gritted his teeth at the million-dollar Colonial, and shoved down the cover to his laptop. Sure, he was financially sound, comfortable even, but did she miss the elaborate house, the fancy restaurants, expensive beauty treatments? Would she tire of the quiet lifestyle she'd chosen? Was the one she led before enough of a lure to send her packing with Matthew? His insides churned.

The dog had jumped on the couch, and Matthew roughly nudged her off. Heat rose up Damien's face and neck. He didn't trust someone who didn't like dogs. Not that he'd entertain the idea of liking him, even if he hadn't eyed Daisy like she was a petri dish swarming with disease. He hated everything this man stood for. He'd taken Lindsey for granted, cut her down emotionally, made her feel small, and left her high and dry when she was the most defenseless. Yet, he was her ex-husband, they'd shared a history, and his mere presence was a threat to Damien. What would he do if she wanted to go with him? Would she expect him to fight for her or stand there defeated?

Damien was glaring at Matthew when Lindsey came back into the room.

"I'd like to wait until we're finally alone, Lindsey, to say what I need to say." Matthew's voice held a hint of a sneer. As if to imply Damien was a lower life-form.

He wanted to say there was no way he was leaving, but this was still her ex-husband and the father of Maris—no matter how miserably he'd failed at both relationships. Damien paused and glanced at Lindsey. The cottage was quiet and the air thick with tension. Lindsey looked down at her hands, and he got a sour taste in his mouth.

Then she lifted her chin and looked Matthew square in the eyes. "Damien lives here. He can decide whether he'd like to come or go."

Pride spread inside his chest. She'd taken the first step to standing up to the man who'd put her down for years. Part of him knew Lindsey had to do this on her own. He wanted to remain beside her on the loveseat, but he also wanted her to know that he believed in her. If he went outside and gave them time to talk, it would be like admitting he not only had confidence in Lindsey, but that he trusted her and the fortitude of their relationship. He needed conviction in what they had as much as she needed to trust herself. Damien squeezed her shoulder. "You've got this," he whispered as he leaned in and kissed her cheek.

Across from them, Matthew flinched away from the dog who'd settled at his feet. Damien snickered lightly and slid off the couch. "I'm going to take this germ beast for a walk. I'll be just outside."

In the kitchen, he found Daisy's leash and clipped it to her collar. Her nails clicked against the wood floors as she pranced in a circle at his feet.

"We're not going far, girl," he muttered to the dog, who was already pawing at the door.

He opened the slider, and closed only the screen, just in case Lindsey needed to holler for backup. Damien tried to concentrate on pitching the yellow tennis ball to Daisy, the fresh air misting his skin, and the toss and turn of the sea—anything to ease the silly thoughts racing through his head. What if Lindsey decided being with Matthew was the best thing for her and Maris? Sure, Matthew was a son of a bitch, but had Damien really treated Lindsey that much better in the past few weeks? He bent down to pick up the ball, and squeezed it hard inside his palm. They'd squabbled and fought over stupid things. Well, maybe not so stupid. He'd messed up taking the painting and again when he stormed out over the letter. Damien cursed himself. He should have done better for her.

A soft breeze caressed his cheek, cleansing away the self-doubt that welled up inside him. A few sailboats dotted the horizon under a bright sun. Waves rolled up the sand and took away the seaweed and debris that cluttered the shore. The Cape was no longer a place of fear and hopelessness for him. It was never the location that had hurt him; his parents had. Lindsey wasn't like his mother. She was brave and kind beyond measure, and would never leave what they had for a few monetary comforts, because this place had healed her too, and Matthew no longer had a hold over her. Some of the heaviness that settled over him dissipated like morning fog burning off on a hot day.

Damien walked closer to the water, and Daisy dropped her ball and followed at his heels. He sat down in the sand, and with the solid beach beneath him, he whispered, "I forgive you." The words that left his lips were whisked away in the wind and replaced by empowerment. By forgiving his parents, not just saying it but really feeling it, he was no longer their victim. Daisy climbed into his lap and licked his chin. He smiled and laughed, feeling full of hope and possibility.

He glanced over his shoulder at the sound of the slider opening and saw Lindsey and Matthew coming onto the deck. Her posture was straight and full of confidence while

Matthew's was wilted. Damien turned back toward the sea and stroked the dog's glossy coat. She needed to have her own moment of power, just as he had had. Maybe on the same day, they could both stop being victims. They could both be freed.

"Matthew, nothing you can say can change my mind. If you're truly interested in playing a role in Maris's life, I would never try to stop you, but moving back to the city with you is not an option. It never will be."

"You'd give up the beautiful home I gave you, the clothes, the trips, to stay in this cardboard box with that Neanderthal? Men like that don't stick, Lindsey. He's playing you because you're naive and available. He's just letting you warm his bed until the next best thing walks by."

"You're describing yourself, Matthew. I choose Damien. You may be Maris's biological father, but he's the father that's nurtured her since birth. I feel sorry for you, Matthew, because for you everything is about having control and wealth. You're a hollow shell who never sees the value in people, or the beauty around you." Her voice was so victorious, Damien's grin stretched ear-to-ear. "I don't hate you anymore, Matthew. Every time you put me down or made me feel like I wasn't good enough was because of your flaws, not mine. I've said what I needed to, now I'm going to spend this lovely day on the beach with Damien and Maris."

"Yes," he quietly cheered from his spot in the sand. Lindsey had triumphed and he couldn't have been prouder of her.

Footsteps sounded on the deck and crunched across the shell drive. When the BMW's engine purred to life, Damien stood up and strode to the deck. Lindsey met him with a big hug at the top of the stairs.

"You did it, and you were amazing," he said as he kissed her forehead.

Lindsey smiled brightly and for a moment they just basked in each other's eyes.

"Can we sit out for a minute? I just want to enjoy you and this feeling for a moment." Lindsey viewed the baby monitor before sitting down at the picnic table they'd put outside. "A day we were both dreading turned out to be pretty good, huh?"

"You have no idea," he said and ran his hand over her cheek. "Lindsey, I haven't been upfront with you in our relationship, and I didn't realize it until you were in there with your ex, that I need to do a better job of showing you, of telling you." He was already fighting to find the words. Communication had never been his strength. But for her, he tried.

"How so?" Lindsey asked, her eyes never leaving his.

Damien laced his free hand with hers, so they were completely connected. He liked the warmth and strength he found in her solid grip. It steadied him. His brows furrowed in concentration. He had to get it right.

"I'm not just here to pass the time. You know that, right?" When Lindsey nodded, he continued. "There's something about spending my days with you and Maris that makes me feel whole. You're both so important to me…" He rubbed his thumbs over her knuckles. Sweat beaded on his forehead. "I've never had as much faith in one person, as I have in you. I trust you Lindsey, like I've never trusted anyone before." Her expression sank and she glanced down at the table. Had he said something wrong? He didn't have a chance to ask before she was getting up.

"Wait here," Lindsey disappeared inside. When she returned, she was carrying a file and gripped it in both hands like it might fall and shatter. Lindsey sat at the table and faced him with unsteady eyes.

"I didn't want you to finish what you were saying, about trust, without knowing. I'm afraid I've made an awful mistake." She let out a breath and scooted the file toward him. "I found her, Damien."

His insides turned to ice. Everything that had been on the cusp of his lips vanished into thin air. "You mean my sister, don't you?" His voice was unsteady. He loved her, and she had betrayed his trust, just like everyone else he'd ever cared for. Damien was rooted to the picnic bench, frozen. It was more than the betrayal. Every blood relative he'd known had left him with invisible scars that never truly healed. He was afraid of more disappointment, more pain, after he'd just found his strength sitting on the beach. Now, Lindsey had resurfaced the trauma he'd just laid to rest.

When he spoke, his voice was so low, he could barely

hear himself. A wave of sickness coiled in his gut. "I told you I didn't want to find her."

"I know, and I'm so sorry for being dishonest, for not letting you make the decision on your own. But if you'll just open the file and look, you'll see she's so much like you—strong and determined. She looks like you, too."

Her voice turned to static in his ears, like he was standing under the engine of a roaring fighter jet. Damien was in shock at what she'd done, and her actions tore at him. Didn't she understand what this meant? He'd already taken a huge leap of faith in himself to build a relationship with Lindsey despite his past. He didn't want all this responsibility and he didn't want someone else he could end up hurting like his parents had hurt him. What if his sister was a living, breathing version of his father or mother? It would suck him back into the vortex of hell he endured the first eighteen years of his life.

"I trusted you." He laughed bitterly. "How was I so wrong about you?"

"I never would have done it to hurt you. I just wanted you to be happy, to have a family of your own. Just like how you wanted me to be successful with my artwork. I was upset when you took the painting without telling me, but in the end, it's brought so many wonderful things." She tried to grasp his hand and he pulled away.

She had earned his trust by treading gently when they went through papers from his father's house. Now the trust they had was built on a lie, too. Lindsey had only pretended to respect his privacy. His pulse was speeding like a race car. He believed her when she said she wouldn't pursue finding his sister. What the hell had happened?

"Lindsey, I get that you did what you thought would be good for me," he said, fighting for control. "That you were trying to give me a family, but I had already found that in you and Maris. I was just about to bare my soul to you." He shook his head and looked her in the eyes. "I love you. I love Maris. How could you lie to me after all we've done to find truth and peace, together?"

They were silent for a moment and the space between them snapped with bitter disappointments.

"I had wanted to build a life with you." His voice cracked as their relationship unraveled like yarn.

"And we still can. Before you say anything else, there's something I need to tell you. It's about your mother." When she reached across the table and tried to take his hand, he flinched away.

"Forget her. You made me believe there was good in people again." He stood up from the picnic table, putting more distance between them. "With you, it was like I could finally stop running and just be." He crossed his arms over his chest and looked out at the shore.

"Damien, please just listen—"

"You were my chance at more than just happiness." His throat was so tight, he could hardly croak out the words.

"You were the family I was supposed to be able to trust and count on. Christ, Lindsey, I wanted to marry you. Have brothers and sisters for Maris." He watched her draw in a sharp breath and place her hand over her mouth. The whole life he'd built up in his mind was pouring out at his feet, like a sack of grain that had been sliced open with a sickle. Lindsey started to rise from the table, tears in her eyes. Her sadness broke him just as much as her deception.

"If I can't trust you, we could never start a life together. You of all people should know what that means to me. I never had trust with my parents, and look where that got me—abandoned by one and beaten senseless by the other." All this time he'd been worried he would hurt Lindsey, but the second he turned, she put a knife in his back.

"I'm not your parents. You know I'm nothing like them. You're just trying to throw me into the same category, so you can run. My mistake makes it easier for you to leave me and Maris, because all along you've been afraid of committing, haven't you?"

Her words seared into him, like a hot iron rod jammed down his throat. "Afraid of committing? I've been all in every step of the way. I might not be Maris's biological father, but goddammit, I'm her father in all the ways that count." What happened now? Would he still get to see her or would he miss out on all the special milestones that were to come? "You didn't just damage our relationship, but the one I'd wanted to build with Maris." He shook his head, letting the full weight of her actions fall on his shoulders. "I thought things would be different with you." He rounded the picnic table and walked straight past her.

Damien gripped the file tightly and went inside. He couldn't leave without seeing Maris one last time. How could he walk away from the child he'd loved from the second he laid eyes on her? How could he stay when sadness and distress coursed through his veins like poison? He glanced in at Maris, who was just starting to stir. Damien walked into the room and ran his fingers over her silky, soft hair. When he whispered goodbye, his heart constricted in his chest. He had to get away from here. The pain was burning holes through him, like Icarus when he'd flown too close to the sun. Damien stuffed some of his belongings inside his backpack, and took his keys of the dresser. Lindsey was standing in the kitchen, hugging her elbows.

"Damien," she said. There was a hint of wild desperation in her voice. He hated the instant urge to soothe her when her chin wobbled.

"There's nothing more to say," he said, and to prove to himself he could, Damien walked out the front door without looking behind him. He jammed the file in his backpack, cursing when the zipper got caught on the cardstock. Footsteps pounded the ground behind him and hands gripped his arm. He turned, and Lindsey was inches from his face. Her eyes glistened with anger and her hair whipped wildly in the wind.

"Don't walk away like this. Please, I'm so sorry." She looked at him through glassy eyes.

"I lost you once when we were kids. I can't let it happen again."

"You should have thought of that before you decided I was too stupid to make my own decisions. If you cared about me, you would've talked to me first. I can't believe I've fallen so hard when I don't even know you." Lindsey sucked in a breath. She looked as if he'd slapped her.

He got on his bike and tore out of the driveway. The entire ride into town, he was keenly aware of the file that was folded inside his backpack. Lindsey had left him with a hard choice. He could discard the file and always wonder what it contained, or he could open it, and risk having more of his heart torn out.

Damien had made a fool of himself by telling Lindsey he loved her. She clearly didn't think as much of him, or she never would have made such a powerful move against his will. Was he some kind of charity case to her? Poor Damien from the wrong side of the tracks, who can't figure his life out on his own. She hadn't treated him as an equal when she'd made the decision to find his sister, but someone who thought they knew what was best for his well-being. It made his heart ache, that she thought less of him, just like Matthew thought less of her. Lindsey of all people should've valued the importance of being a team, and of playing on a level field. Damien pulled his bike into an empty spot in front of the Seahorse Inn. He pressed the heel of his hand against his sternum, trying to ease the pain there.

Damien had grossly misjudged Lindsey, and now he'd have to pay for it with the crushing disappointment that pounded in his chest and a belly tangled full of sickening knots. He grabbed one of the double door handles that was carved into the shape of a seahorse. A blast of conditioned air hit him in the face. He was so numb, it barely registered.

"Welcome to the Seahorse Inn. It's a beautiful day in Chatham, isn't it?" Great. Marcia-Fucking-Brady wanted to chat. He needed isolation like a fish needed water.

"I need a room, please," he said and pushed his anger down. It wasn't the employee's fault he had the floor ripped from under his feet.

"Certainly, sir. It's your lucky day. We have one room left," she chirped. "How long will you be staying?"

"Just tonight." He'd already pulled out his credit card and slid it across the desk. She took the hint and quietly swiped it, keyed two plastic room cards, and folded them into an envelope.

"We have a lovely hot breakfast every morning beginning at seven."

"Great, thanks," he said and was halfway down the hallway before she could get another word out.

He slid his key card into the door, a green light flashed, and the door handle gave way. It was ironic there was vacancy, now that his relationship with Lindsey had torn apart in a Bermuda Triangle of dishonesty.

He threw his backpack on the bed and sat on the corner. He let his head fall into his hands as he absorbed the shock of what had happened. It took all his energy to ignore the ominous file inside the tiny room, like a great white shark floating through a backyard swimming pool. He took a shower to wash away the day. It only reminded him of the steamier ones he and Lindsey had shared. Once again, he found himself completely and utterly alone. Maybe fate was trying to tell him something—that there wasn't meant to be another set of footprints in the sand beside his. Finally, he fell into bed, letting thoughts of Lindsey drift into oblivion as he tossed into a restless sleep.

Chapter Sixteen

"Is Jason Hall available?" Lindsey bit her bottom lip as she stood at the front desk of Veterans' Services. The secretary raised her brow over her bright green eye glasses.

"I'd be happy to check for you. Who should I tell him is visiting?"

"Lindsey Hunter." This was a stupid idea. She was just dragging one more person into their personal problems but she was hanging onto a tether of sanity. For the past twenty-four hours since he'd left, she'd paced and analyzed, chewed her nails so short they stung, and crawled through the motions of motherhood—which only added more to the guilt stew rolling to a boil inside her. Thank God her parents agreed to watch Maris for a few hours while she sorted things out.

"Mr. Hall would be happy to see you. He's just finishing up with a client," the woman said.

Lindsey walked into the waiting room and caught a glimpse of her reflection in the long mirror hanging on the wall. No wonder the secretary gave her a once-over. She looked like she'd just crawled off the set of *The Walking*

Dead—like literally up from the dirt as a zombie. Her face was ashen, and she had rabid raccoon eyes—red with dark rings below, from day-old mascara and too many tears. It didn't matter, she needed to find some connection to Damien, someone who might know where he'd gone. She'd pulled in the lot expecting to see his bike there. Did he quit his job? Had he acted that fast in an effort to put miles between them? Lindsey couldn't spend day after painstaking day wondering if it was truly over. Her stomach turned and her heart leaped up to her throat.

A child's laughter filled the waiting room and Lindsey looked up to see Jay escorting a family out. A little sandy-haired girl clutching a red balloon dog tipped her chin up at Jay. "Thank you, Mister Jason, for the puppy." Her eyes sparkled in admiration.

"Next time we'll make a balloon monkey. I've been practicing." Jay winked at her and turned to the parents. "Thanks for coming in. Let me know if you have any hitches with the new program."

"You've been a real help, Jason." The man and woman with the little girl shook Jay's hand and walked out of the office building.

Once they'd left, Jay strode toward Lindsey. "Hey, is everything okay?" he asked. Genuine concern coursed through his voice. "You look—"

"Like a zombie. I'm very much aware." She gestured to the mirror behind them and Jay chuckled.

"I was thinking Frodo after he crossed middle-earth, weighed down by an evil ring." He offered her a sympathetic grin.

"Gee, thanks," she said with no real emotion behind it. How could she care how she looked when she'd hurt Damien so badly? She didn't deserve him, but Maris did.

He held out his hand to her, and she took it. "What I meant is you look like you've been through hell. Why don't you come back and we can talk in private?"

She nodded and he led her down the hall to his office. "Take a seat, I'll be right back."

He disappeared and she was left alone in a modest office. One simple cedar desk was flanked by two deeply cushioned chairs. In the corner, he had a child-sized table with coloring books, crayons, and stickers. Someone had recently been at them, because Ana, Elsa, and Olaf were plastered to the carpet and wall. Jay didn't seem like the type to be rattled by a few stickers, though. He popped back through the doorway carrying a tray of tea and cookies.

"I have sisters. I know how this works," he said passing her a cup of steaming water. Lindsey chose a tea bag, unwrapped it, and let it seep in.

"If they don't appreciate you, I'm an only child looking to adopt a brother." Lindsey bent her face closer to the mug, letting the bergamot scented steam comfort her.

Jay laughed. "I'll let them know I'm being pursued, and maybe one of them will make me dinner tonight. So, did something happen with you and Damien?" He chose the seat next to her, instead of behind the desk.

"I made a mess of everything." Lindsey held her mug with both hands and glanced into the water.

"We all do from time to time." He leaned toward her, ready to listen.

"We had a fight and he left. I came here expecting to find him, but his bike wasn't in the lot. Did he quit Veterans' Services?"

"No, but he did request a personal day." Some of the thickness in her throat dissipated. Maybe there was hope after all. Lindsey had so many feelings for Damien that were left unsaid, and they were drilling a hole through her heart. He'd said he loved her. But did he mean the words to drive the hurt deeper? She had to find out, because she loved him too. After a childhood of hearing neither of those things, it would be important for him to know. As much as she dreaded the thought, she had an obligation to tell him about his mother's death, too.

"Rarely are things so broken they can't be fixed," Jay said quietly.

She wasn't sure if it was his calming nature, or listening ear, but words started spilling out of Lindsey's mouth like a tipped glass of milk. "Do you remember Alex? The woman that joined us for dinner?" Jay nodded and she noticed a spark lit in his eyes. "She runs a very successful PI firm and I had her track down Damien's sister, who he didn't realize he even had until I found a letter while we were cleaning out items from his father's house."

"Hmm. And Damien didn't want to find her, right?" Lindsey's head jerked up.

"I hadn't realized he told you." How much did Jay know about Damien and his past?

"He didn't tell me what happened between the two of you, but I can understand why meeting his sister would shake him. Between his background check and the bits and pieces he's told me, I know he's experienced trauma. In his childhood, and then in the Marines. It's harder for victims to face their past. Meeting his sister might be like reliving whatever he'd experienced again."

Oh, God, how could she fix this? Lindsey swallowed. Her throat was bone dry despite the tea. Would she ever be able to erase the pained look on his face from her mind—complete betrayal and irrevocable anger? She needed to see him to tell him all those things that tangled her up in knots—that she loved him and could picture being with him year after year. She wanted more little feet stomping around the house, too, maybe not right now but definitely in the future. What she did was dead-wrong and even if he wouldn't take her back she needed to apologize and tell him what he meant to her.

"I need to try to make this right, or at least apologize for hurting him. Can you tell me where he is?" She held her breath, hoping and praying that he knew. She hung on to the warm mug of tea, trying to fight the cold that swept through her fingers.

"He didn't say, but I thought I saw his bike in front of the inn downtown." Could he be that close? Hope skyrocketed to the tiled ceiling.

"Thank you so much." She stood up and set the cup down on the tray.

"Good luck. I'll be rooting for you guys." Jay stood up with her, picked up her purse, and handed it to her.

She hesitated, then rose up on her tippy toes to kiss his scarred cheek.

Jay squeezed her shoulder. "You make him happy. You and Maris." She hadn't done a very good job of it lately. Her eyes burned. If only she just left things alone.

Lindsey rushed out before the tears started to fall. She took the elevator to the first floor, got in her car, and drove toward the direction of the Seahorse Inn. She had been so wrong to try to push him together with his sister, thinking his sibling might help to heal his past. Damien had hit the nail on the head during their fight. *As far as family goes, I thought that's what we were.* His words stripped the thoughts out of her head, and made her forget why she'd contacted Alex in the first place.

Damien didn't understand how a family worked. Had he been so afraid of being left, that he did the leaving first? Just like his mother had to him? Lindsey had to show him when a solid family screwed up, they fought to stay together. They compromised, made sacrifices, and talked it out. They didn't high tail it in the opposite direction. Damien was family to her. Family to Maris. He was the closest thing her child had to a father and she was prepared to fight for him and the relationship they both deserved.

If one of them had to steer the ship, she'd take the helm. Lindsey was done letting others control her destiny. She wanted Damien in her life, and she wouldn't let him walk out for the second time so easily. He'd hear her out long enough for her to make her point crystal clear. Damien could brood for days, even months, over the decision she'd made. But if there was an ounce of love in him for her and Maris, she'd do everything in her power to get him home to them.

Sure, she was mad at his reaction to the news but she'd half expected it, and braced herself for it. Part of her worried the taking off would become a pattern, that he'd end up leaving her like his mother had left him. The other part of her had enough faith in the man he'd become, to know he'd do right by them. It was a level of trust he didn't under-stand—or didn't think the people in his life were capable of. He was betrayed by her actions, but if she hadn't believed in him, she wouldn't have made such a big step on his behalf. Damien was strong enough to shoulder a meeting with his sister. He'd come out better for it.

She pulled into one of the vacant spots lining the street, and glanced up and down the road. Her heart dipped.

Damien's bike was nowhere to be seen. Still, she got out of the car and entered the lobby where Damien had tried to find a room on the very first night they reconnected. She supposed she owed the Seahorse Inn for rekindling their relationship. If he'd been able to stay here, Damien might have gone along his business of arranging the funeral and cleaning out the house on his own. They never would've been able to build a relationship like they had.

"Excuse me, miss," Lindsey asked the young girl at the front desk. "May I send a call up to Damien Trent's room, please?"

The girl trailed a nectarine-colored nail down a large book sitting in front of her, and glanced up, eyes full of apology. "I'm sorry, Mr. Trent checked out just a few hours ago."

Lindsey's shoulders drooped. She was too late. He'd put distance between them and his message was clear. Much like he hadn't wanted her to find his sister, he didn't want to be found, either. After thinking about what she was going to say to him, rehearsing it to herself in the mirror, she was utterly deflated, like building a glorious sand castle only to have it washed away by the tide. What would Damien do now? Go back to the Marines, put as many zip codes between them as possible? If he continued to work at Veterans' Services, she'd have to tiptoe around the downtown area. It would be crushing to constantly run into him. Would Damien ever meet his sister, or did she dissolve their relationship over a few photos and records that would never be seen?

"Ma'am," the girl waived her hand in front of Lindsey's face. "Is there something else I can help you with?"

Heat rose to Lindsey's cheeks. She wasn't sure how long she'd been standing at the front desk with the girl's words falling on deaf ears.

"No, thank you, though," she said and walked back to her car. Once she was inside the enclosed space, she let the first hot tear slide down her cheek. It blazed the trail for hundreds of others that seemed to burst freely from the flood gates. Lindsey slumped down and rested her head on the steering wheel; her earlier bravado sapped.

Maybe they'd both misplaced their trust. She suddenly doubted everything, including the feelings she thought Damien had for her. How could he throw everything away so easily? What was worse, he'd walked away from Maris, too. He was the second man to leave Maris in her short life, and it hurt worse than being left herself. Would Maris ever know a father figure? How could he let go of the child he'd helped raise since she was first born? When he had spoken to Maris, there had been love and tenderness in his voice. Had she imagined it out of her own blissful thinking? Lindsey supposed this was a blessing in disguise. It would've been so much worse if Maris was old enough to comprehend the situation.

Providing a stable, loving home for Maris meant far more than catering to her own feelings. From now on, it would be just the two of them. Whatever remaining belief she had in happily ever after, had been zapped right out of her. Would she ever have what her parents had? They were entering thirty-three years of marriage and she'd blown through one marriage and serious relationship in three years. Was there something wrong with her that made men leave or stray, some personality flaw? With Matthew, she'd been too weak and let him manipulate every situation. With Damien, maybe she'd been too hardheaded, and took control of contacting Alex when it was Damien's decision to do so.

Maybe it was possible for others to find ever-after, but not for her. She had more than enough love between her sweet child and her parents. The lie was meant to comfort, but a fresh wave of tears shook her. There would always be something missing without Damien. Every time she looked at the nursey he'd designed for Maris, or strolled by the auto shop on Main Street she'd remember, and be faced with what-ifs. Lindsey pulled herself together, started the ignition, and tried desperately to leave thoughts of Damien behind.

Chapter Seventeen

DAMIEN HAD DRIVEN off the Cape like a man possessed. The coastal grass and marshy bogs had been a blur of green and gold at the corners of his eyes. Lindsey had betrayed him. Endless cups of stale coffee had left a gnawing hole churning in his stomach. He wanted to drink himself into oblivion, but he was better than that. He'd read his sister's file. She was born in withdrawals. No, he was nothing like the people that gave him life. It finally clicked for him. No matter how hard he tried, he could never be as selfish as they had been. He was hard on himself, and he'd been an asshole these past few days, but he was a decent human being. One that could actually put others before himself. One that was able to say no to mind-numbing substances because they could threaten the people he loved. Despite the disadvantages they'd caused him, he'd turned out better than his father. An addict. Better than his mother, who had his baby sister in a doped-up stupor.

The file had taken on a life of its own, beckoning to him throughout the night until finally he threw off the sheets and sat at the work desk. He'd deliberated for nearly an hour with streams of endless scenarios playing through his head. When he finally got the guts to open it, the wind whooshed out of his lungs. The face staring back at him was a fresh and healthy version of his mother's. Their mother's. He spent the remainder of the night poring over the documentation, which included everything from report cards to medical records. Each one he read softened him to the girl—his sister. Maybe he was wrong about her. Lindsey's words replayed over and over.

"What if she's sweet and kind? Someone you'd grow to love? Damien, you could have a wonderful family member out there, and you're brushing her aside. What if she needs you, too?"

Maybe that was the reason he stood at the gates of Boston University, because as much as he wanted to leave the past where it belonged, his sister had struggled, too. Kate was hurt by the same people as he had been. Lindsey hadn't left him a choice. It was a terrible thing, to have something so big, so important be stripped from your hands. He looked at the double doors of the main campus. What was he supposed to do, lurk outside like some stalker, on the off chance his sister walked through the building? And what then? How did you explain something like this to someone you've never met?

Hairs tingled on the back of his neck. He was being watched. Damien turned his head to the left and there she was, sitting with a birch tree against her back and books spread around her knees. She held his gaze with eyes he knew would be as blue as his own. She shifted to her knees, gathered the books, and stood up. Kate walked toward him. It could have been seconds, or years, he wasn't sure. He stood stiffly with his hands tucked tight inside his jean pockets. Then she was in front of him. Her eyes flashed, something hard and sad swarmed behind her lids. She dropped the backpack at his feet, and crushed her arms around his shoulders. How could she possibly know who he was? What did it matter?

In her embrace he found complete acceptance, and an innocence that turned him into the lowest of creatures for wanting to live his life without knowing her at all. Kate stepped back and looked up at him.

"You have my face," she whispered. "My mother told me, the day before she died, that you existed. I thought it was the high talking, but now you're here."

If he were hit by an eighteen-wheeler, the blow would have been softer than the words she delivered. Lindsey had mentioned his mother during their fight. She'd tried to tell him. They were orphans.

"Oh, my God." She stepped forward and clutched his shoulder. "I'm such an idiot. You didn't know. Of course you wouldn't have known." When tears threatened to spring from her eyes, he shook his head.

"It's okay." He repeated the words again, until her face softened. "We have a lot of catching up to do. It won't all be pleasant."

Kate blew out a breath, sending her choppy side bang flying up. "A lifetime." She grabbed his hand, easy and trusting. "You found me and now we have each other...except, I don't know your name." She looked up and studied his face.

"Damien," he said. Could it be that simple? How could she accept him into her life with the snap of a finger? "Hungry? Maybe we could grab a bite, talk a bit?" Damien wanted to do the right thing, he wanted to try. He lifted her backpack, and slung it over his shoulder.

She nodded. "I know a place up the street. Burgers the size of your head, dripping with grease. Perfect for a family reunion." Leading him by the hand, she tugged him up a few blocks. They rounded a corner and stepped into Jake's Shake Shack. The smell of fried food made his stomach grumble. He couldn't remember the last time he'd eaten. They slid into a cherry-red booth in the back of the restaurant and ordered drinks, cherry vanilla soda for her, and a water to cool the perpetual ache in his throat.

"When did it happen?" The question rendered him breathless, but he had to ask. He unwrapped a straw and popped it in his drink.

"She was in and out of rehab my whole life. It was like this all-consuming demon she couldn't break free of. I tried to help, I swear it, but I was just so tired. Tired of calling the ambulance, tired of the hospitals, of the bills. It was the week I gave her the ultimatum. Get clean, or I won't see you ever again." Kate swiped a tear from her cheek and Damien's chest crushed inside him. "I got the call the next day. She'd overdosed in rehab, of all places."

He couldn't think of the right words to say. He now knew what had driven his mother to leave. Had his father tried to help her get clean? He'd never really thought of his father's own struggle. It must have been a lot to have a young wife who was addicted to heroin. Maybe he gave her an ultimatum, too, and forced her to leave him behind. Were all the beatings and harsh words a result of his pain, or not knowing how to raise an unruly boy? It didn't make it right and it didn't fix things, but it gave him a new perspective.

"And our father?" Kate twisted and knotted a straw wrapper. It looked like his insides, after days of stress.

"He died of complications from alcohol abuse. I enlisted the second I graduated high school and didn't look back. Maybe I could've done something."

"Don't. If you're anything like me, you've been forced to play the blame game your whole life." She looked up at him, a young girl, with eyes of an old soul. "We're together, and that's something happy."

The waitress came back and dropped two overflowing baskets in front of them. A grin ghosted around Kate's mouth and two dimples popped on her cheeks. "I'm going to go ahead and bury my sorrows in this giant burger. I suggest you do the same, or I'm coming for it." As if to prove her point, she picked it up with both hands and lifted it to her mouth. She took a giant bite that turned her little cheeks into a chipmunk's.

He laughed. "No way you could eat two of these things. I think I'm safe." Damien liked her sense of humor and quick smile. Lindsey was right—she'd been through a lot, too, and she was built tough. He admired that.

"They used to have a free food policy for employees at the diner I work at. They changed it when I came around." Kate took a break from the burger to gulp down some soda. They got there at the right time because every red vinyl seat in the restaurant and at the counter was taken. Every few minutes a new plate appeared in the kitchen window as the cook churned out orders.

With each laugh Kate and Damien shared, something eased and released inside his soul. Maybe things would be okay after all. If only he hadn't screwed up so badly with Lindsey, things would really be looking up. The sterile manila file she gave to him was supposed to lend to stress and pain. Did Lindsey give him a gift instead? When enthusiasm lit up his sister's eyes as she told him all about college and what she was majoring in, he second-guessed his anger and the biting words that spilled off his tongue at Lindsey. Had Lindsey known exactly what she was doing? And if she did, she must have known he'd fly off the handle and leave, but she did it anyway. Did she believe so deeply in the power of family, that she'd risk what they'd built to make sure he had one of his own, no matter how small it was?

Kate cleared her basket, licked the ketchup off her finger, and eyed longingly at the fries still piled on his plate. Damien grinned and slid the basket toward her.

"My sister's a straight-up savage." His heart lifted when she grinned and chuckled. He was glad he came to Boston. "The food must suck at your school."

"Oh, I don't have a dining plan. You have to live on campus for that," she said and popped a fry in her mouth.

"If you don't live on campus, where are you staying?" Damien wasn't sure he wanted to know the answer. Was his little sister homeless?

"In Mom's apartment—really my apartment since I could earn a paycheck. Do you think you could give me a lift, when we're done?"

"Of course," he said. What type of apartment could a college student afford in the middle of a major metropolitan city? He was impressed by her ability to juggle so many different plates. If he hadn't enlisted, he would've been finding trouble. His sister was a scholar and a hard worker at such a young age.

"Do you have a family of your own?" Kate asked. "A wife or a girlfriend?"

"I had one. A girlfriend. It didn't work out." It hurt to say the words. To openly admit they were no longer together.

"What happened?" Kate said, wide eyes filled with curiosity.

"She did something—" Damien stopped himself. What was he going to say? That she did something he couldn't forgive? He looked at the girl sitting in front of him. His blood. His sister. Saying he couldn't forgive Lindsey for introducing them would be like saying his sister was some awful mistake. That he'd never wanted her in the first place. "We had a disagreement, and I don't think she'll be forgiving me anytime soon."

Kate rolled her eyes, and looked impossibly youthful for all she'd been through. "Well how do you know she won't, if you don't try?"

"I said some pretty rotten stuff," he admitted. He was so scared of what she'd found; he was spouting off words in angry bursts. He didn't deserve to be a shell caught in the tread of her sneakers.

Kate flapped her hand as if to brush his comment aside. "People say words they don't mean. It's the actions that count. Words can be twisted or faked, actions can't." There was that old soul thing again.

"Maybe you have a point." The bill came and Damien plucked it off the table, pulled out his wallet, and stacked a few bills neatly on top of the slip. When they stepped outside, Kate linked arms with him. The gesture made his heart melt. They walked back to campus, and got on his bike.

"Where to?" Damien asked. Kate gave him an address and then shouted directions over the wind and noise as they

187

blew through the city. The scenery began to change from quaint brownstones and glass high-rises, to crowded triple-deckers lined tighter than a row of dominos. She shouted to turn right and yelled out a building number. Graffiti washed the buildings and a few chained-up dogs barked outside them. A woman walked around the corner, her barely-there dress revealing bony legs and skyscraper heels. She leaned into the passenger side of a car window, deliberated, then slid in. Damien gritted his teeth. His baby sister had grown up in the slums and now she lived here alone. He'd known her only a few hours, but he wanted better for her. He would give her better. The sun had escaped below the city line by the time he parked his bike.

"I'd take everything you have inside," Kate said and fished through her backpack for a set of keys.

"Can I take the bike, too?" he said only half joking.

They pushed past a group of men sitting on the warped steps of the building smoking, and squeezed inside. They walked up the stairs leaving a trail through the dust every time either of them gripped the railing. He was completely confident that the building wouldn't pass a fire inspection. She stopped in front of a door, and slid her key in the lock. There were shouts above them. His eyes darted toward the ceiling. Something shattered, and then went quiet. This was not a nice place. Damien followed her into the apartment, and Kate shut the door, fastening several locks that went around the frame. Inside was worn down, but she'd made it bright, cheery, and clean with colorful pillows on the couch and red valances in the windows.

"You stay here, alone?" he asked again. "It doesn't seem like the safest neighborhood, Kate."

"What clued you in?" She laughed his question off, then turned to him when he continued to stare at her with concern. "It's my home Damien. For now, it's what I have."

He couldn't dispute that, but she wouldn't be staying here alone tonight. An intense need to protect her from any more harm or hurt made him want to drive her away from this place. Kate agreed to let him crash on the couch and brought out a pile of blankets and pillows. They stayed up late, chatting about everything and nothing. He told her about Lindsey and Maris, and eventually what their fight had been about. She understood he was scared to meet her, but told him how glad she was he'd found her. When the clock ticked past midnight, she padded down the hall to her room for bed.

Wailing sirens and the mad bark of dogs kept him up. He got up once, then twice to check the locks on the door. Damien lay on the lumpy couch and put his hands behind his head. Lindsey had broken his trust, betrayed his heart, and reconnected him with his little sister who he had an instant bond with. Could he ever thank her enough for pushing him off the ledge with one swift kick? She had wanted him to have a piece of his family, and Kate was the best part of what could have been growing up. He tried to picture what their life would be like now, and could image Kate there, but also Lindsey and Maris. They had become his family, too. That wasn't something you could throw away with a single disagreement or fight. Lindsey and Maris were his and he'd run away. He was always afraid of being like his mother, and in trying not to be, ended up doing the exact same thing.

Damien's chest tightened. What if it was already too late? He was just starting to figure his life out, one that revolved around this new beautiful family and he'd tossed part of it away in an angry rage. He sat up and rubbed the back of his neck. Would he be a good partner to Lindsey—a good father to Maris, long-term? If he kept second-guessing himself, he'd never get anywhere. He loved them enough to do what it took. Damien knew at that moment he had to fight for them. Kate was right, if Lindsey was going to forgive him, he needed to show her with actions. A grand gesture to prove to her he wasn't playing around. He wanted her and Maris for keeps.

Damien swallowed hard. The inside of his mouth was suddenly as dry as old bread. Lindsey could turn him away. Would she forgive him? Had Matthew already swooped in to pick up the pieces? Damien gritted his teeth and glanced at the clock. He'd give an arm and a leg for the hands to tick by faster. Damien stood up and paced the living room. He needed to see Lindsey's face, and to touch her soft skin. He needed to look into her eyes, and see that everything was okay. If only he phoned her before he left, texted even. Had she looked for him? If she found out he'd left town, would she think he'd abandoned her and the baby? The back of his throat burned. That's exactly what he'd done. Damien was so preoccupied and out of his mind with fear of the past, that he'd walked away from the two most important things in his life, without a second glance. *What an ass.*

He swiped his hand over his head. Never again. He'd set things right. He had to. Damien reached for his cell phone. He might still be upset that Lindsey had been untruthful, but that didn't mean he wasn't thinking about them. *Are you okay?* He tapped in the message before he could change his mind.

The phoned pinged almost instantly. *Not really, are you?*

Damien sat back on the couch. *Not really.*

You had every right to react the way you did. I'm just asking for a chance to explain. Can we talk this through? Damien reread Lindsey's text a second and third time. Instead of blaming him for running off, she was faulting herself for everything.

There are a few things I need to take care of, but I'll come by later in the day. Kiss Maris for me.

Already did. The text made him want to smile and cry at the same time.

Damien rested his head in his palms. He missed his girls.

SOFT FOOTPRINTS TIPTOED over the wood floors and

Damien looked up from the stove. Kate stretched her arms high over her head, yawned, and walked over to the coffee-maker.

"Are you cooking breakfast, big brother?" She tilted her head to the side and peered into the skillet. Unable to sleep past the crack of dawn, Damien had untethered a skillet, and cracked a few eggs into the pan.

"I thought if I buttered you up with breakfast, you'd help me with something today. I screwed up everything with Lindsey, and you're right, actions speak louder than words. I need her to know I'm committed to her and the baby one hundred percent."

Kate's face perked up and she clapped her hands together. "Oh, Damien! You're going to propose. I'm so happy for you." She stretched up on her tippy toes and gave him a peck on the cheek. Was it odd he was relieved at his little sister's approval? They'd just met and already her input was important to him.

"I was hoping you could help me with the ring part, being a girl and all. Because it's the weekend, I thought you might like to pack a bag and stay in Chatham for a few days. You can meet Lindsey and Maris. If she doesn't forgive me, though, we'll have to schlep back to Boston." Would it come to that? He scraped most of the eggs onto Kate's plate. His choppy stomach couldn't handle much. Damien set the dish on the table in front of her and took his own plate to sit across from her.

"Don't think that way! You love her and she loves you. There's nothing that can stand in the way of that, even a stupid disagreement. There's nothing I'd like more than to go with you, but I work double shifts at a diner on the weekends." A deep frown sloped across her face. Damien wanted Kate there when he faced Lindsey—or afterward at least…if Lindsey forgave him. He now had three important females in his life, and he wanted them all in one place.

Kate reached her fork over the table to stab up some of his eggs, and he nudged the plate closer to her. "That's something I wanted to talk to you about, too. You can quit the diner, and you can sign up for college housing. I just found you, and I want you to stay safe."

She smiled and shook her head. "Damien, that's sweet, but money doesn't grow on trees."

"I got an email last night. I put our father's house on the market, and it's sold. You're just as entitled to the profits as I am. We'll split it fifty-fifty. It should give you plenty to enroll in housing, get that meal plan, plus some nice padding to put in your savings account or do whatever with." The email had been the only thing to drag him through the endless night of stress. Now he could put that part of his life behind him and move forward with the future.

Her eyes widened and her mouth gaped open. Kate put her fork down quickly. "Damien, that's your money. It wouldn't be fair; I never even met him."

"Then he owes you more. You'll take it because it's your

money, too." He cleared the empty plates and took them to the sink. His lips curved when he heard Kate on the phone, giving her notice to the diner.

Chapter Eighteen

THE GALLERY HAD called Lindsey in for a meeting that morning. Her paintings had sold—not just one or two but every piece they had. The owner wanted more, and he wanted to feature her work on an ongoing basis for his Cape Cod location and for his gallery on Martha's Vineyard. She should be so happy, and on the surface she was, but deep down she was so torn up inside. Lindsey slipped off her patent leather pumps and left them in the sand. Her parents took Maris for the day, so she could meet with the gallery staff. Still outfitted from the occasion, she walked down her stretch of beach, feeling the hem of her dress wisp around her knees.

The day was gray and cool for summer. Lindsey stepped closer to the ocean, letting the surf wash over her feet as she walked. She wanted to share her news with Damien. After all, he'd helped to make it happen. Now, all her dreams were coming true, except for the one where she and Damien shared happily-ever-after. Failing with Matthew had hurt and embarrassed her. Losing Damien left her broken. Spots flickered in her vision. Lindsey faced the ocean and inhaled the heavy sea air. Damien hadn't just walked away—she pushed him.

Her limbs trembled and she hugged her waist. Would he ever trust her again? Sure, he'd texted her last night and seemed willing to talk, but could he really move past what she'd done? Lindsey dug her feet into the wet sand. As much as she screwed up, maybe Damien never planned to stick around anyway, and her mistakes made for an easy exit. Was he waiting for her to slip up and let him down, just like everyone else had? If so, she didn't disappoint. Her chin wobbled. She had been waiting for Damien to disappoint her, too. He had been so good to them—too good to be true, except he was.

She pressed a fist to her chest, and tried to push away the ache. Damien had held her hand during labor, helped her overcome every contraction, and when Maris made her first appearance he was the one to cut the cord and welcome her into the world. She'd never forget the look in his eyes when Maris clutched his pinky finger—he'd simply melted. He had tested her new name, and the syllables slid slowly over his tongue, like he was uttering something precious and beautiful. *It's just right. She's just right.* Damien's words were branded into her memory. The moment had taken her breath. He was right. She'd damaged two relationships when she chose to find Kate. She'd driven a wedge between Maris and a loving father. The wind carried away her whimper.

Damien had created her baby a dream nursery, one that

could have rivaled any magazine spread. It had come from the heart. And when he touched her, kissed her, those moments were real and profound. She'd felt his heart thud wildly against her chest. Tears rolled down her cheeks. She didn't bother to swipe them away. Lindsey stopped. Suddenly she could feel eyes on her back. She turned slowly and knew it would be him before she saw his face.

Her heart tumbled. Her breath stilled inside her throat. Damien was on the beach, only feet behind her. She'd thought of him endlessly since he'd left, and poured over all the things that remained unsaid. Now that he was there, his eyes locked on hers, Lindsey was rendered speechless. What did you say to a man you'd cut to the core, yet wanted to see more than anything else in the entire world?

"I was wrong," he shouted the words to be heard over the waves smashing against the sand. "You told me I wouldn't be able to move forward until I faced my past, and I have. I met my sister." He moved closer, and with each step Lindsey's breath quickened. She was afraid of what he had to say, afraid to hope for the impossible. When he opened his mouth to speak, Lindsey held her breath. "You were wrong, though, too. I already had a family of my own. One comprised of two people who I care about above all else."

Lindsey wanted to go to him, but her feet stayed firmly planted in the sand. The tide was rolling in, and the waves smacked her ankles.

"I told you once before, and it still holds true. I love you,

Lindsey, and I love Maris. You've both wrapped an anchor around my heart."

The words made hope leap into her throat. "Damien, I lost you when we were kids, and again when you left the cottage. I can't set myself up to lose you again, but I know I did a terrible thing by finding your sister against your will. That you had a reason to walk away."

He took a step forward, then another, slowly closing in on her. His eyes held a mix of fear and desperation. Was he afraid of losing her? Afraid of being rejected? Her heart wanted to accept his words, to run into the solid arms that would wrap around her like a safety net.

"I kept telling myself that I searched for your sister to help you, when in reality it was for me all along. I wanted you to connect with her in hopes you'd be able to find closure, and make a future with me and Maris."

"The day your ex visited, I forgave my parents. Forgiving them released a part of me that was still tied up in anger and guilt."

Lindsey nodded as tears dampened her cheeks. "Just like when I stood up to Matthew for the first time. Oh, Damien, I'm so sorry. I took the decision out of your hands and with it the opportunity to heal from the experience. Please forgive me?"

"I screwed up, too, Linds. When I left, I didn't realize it was because I needed to find Kate. All along, in the back of my mind, I knew I was going to open the file and go to her."

"Then maybe, if you're ready, we could try again." She choked out the words and clasped her elbows tightly.

"You deserve better than how I've acted. I already forgave you, and if you'll forgive me too, I'll spend every day working to be the man you and Maris deserve." Damien's voice shook and his feverish eyes searched her face.

"Will you stay on Cape Cod? When your father's house sells, will you want to leave? What if you decide you want to be close to Kate, and move to Boston?" she said.

"The Realtor emailed me last night to let me know the house sold, and I'm standing here. I can visit Kate at school. And who knows where she'll want to move when she graduates? Maybe it will be to Cape Cod. She's never been here before. In fact, she's never even seen the ocean. Her jaw hung open the whole ride here. All she's ever known are the slums of Boston."

Lindsey's brows knitted together. "She's here?" Had he brought Kate here, to meet her?

"I needed to talk with you alone first. She's waiting in the car." Damien waded through the water to stand directly in front of her. The tide had risen just below her knees and the cold water had goose bumps running up her legs and over her arms. She didn't care.

"Lindsey, do you love me, too?" He stood at arm's length with his hands at his sides.

"The day you stole my lunch box, you stole my heart. I've always loved you, Damien." Water sloshed up her legs as she closed the distance between her and Damien. She placed a hand on either side of his cheeks and pressed gently. "I'm ready to fight for this. For us."

"You told me family is the most important thing, and you're right. Let me be part of your family, Lindsey. Let me be a husband to you and a father to Maris. I can't promise we won't disagree, or that things will be perfect all the time, but together we can make anything work." He stared at her, unblinking, waiting for a response.

When she said nothing, he stepped forward again. He stood so close she could see the worry lines that seemed to pop up on his forehead and face overnight. This hadn't been easy on him, either. He whispered her name, and his voice held a quiet determination. "No more running from problems. No more fear. We have to have trust. Not just in each other but trust that we're always on each other's side. Because both times we've broken trust, it was because we wanted something that the other needed."

Lindsey's heart thumped wildly in her chest. Damien was pouring himself at her feet. He wanted things she'd only wished for on birthday candles and shooting stars. In the middle of the water, he dropped to one knee and her heart jammed into her throat.

The ring in his hand shimmered and sparkled under the afternoon sun that was poking through the clouds.

"Lindsey, will you start a life with me in this cottage by the sea?"

She stepped forward and lifted her hands to the sides of his face. He wasn't playing around this time. He wanted her and Maris. She let the tears stream down her cheeks.

"I'd start a life with you anywhere." Her words were breathless but it was all the encouragement he needed.

Damien slipped the ring on her finger. He stood up, and wrapped her into a hug. Had she ever felt more secure? More loved?

"Lindsey, you gave me a wonderful gift by finding my sister. Kate is warm and sweet—" He stopped mid-sentence and they both turned to the high-pitched squeal from the beach. Kate was standing on an embankment, clapping her hands and doing a little dance.

"I don't mean to spoil the moment, which I caught on camera by the way. I'm just so excited!" Kate shouted down to them. She was already half running, half sliding down the sandy hill.

"She's very bubbly and very enthusiastic. I think you'll love her." Damien's words tickled Lindsey's ear and she couldn't contain her wide grin.

"I know I will." She'd love everything about their life together. Even when things were difficult, they'd make it work, because they'd already weathered the storm together and had come out stronger.

Damien framed her face with his hands and kissed her with the salty waves splashing around their legs and sand beneath their toes. They'd found their way home, together.

Epilogue

I T WAS THE perfect beach day. The sun warmed the sand and water just enough to enjoy it. Behind her, Damien and Kate played volleyball. The rhythmic whack of skin against the inflated plastic, paired with their laughter and friendly insults, touched deep within Lindsey's heart. Damien had found a positive connection to his past, a blood relative he could actually count on and trust—and he found it in spades with his sister. Kate had a car on campus now, and nearly every weekend she drove to Chatham and stayed with them at the cottage.

Lindsey loved having Kate visit. She doted on Maris and filled the house with laughter and fun that only a college student could bring. And then, there was watching Damien and his sister interact. They got along like summer and picnics. If she didn't know better, she would have thought they'd spent a lifetime bonding as siblings—longer than a year, at least.

Beside her, Maris kicked at the water and squealed in the delight each time the cool waves lapped against her wiggling piggy-toes. Even the wide-brimmed hat couldn't shadow her gap-toothed grin. She clapped two chubby hands together and sent a smile toward Lindsey. Drool rolled down her chin. Lindsey draped an arm around Maris's shoulders and squeezed, leaning in so she could breathe in the sunscreen lathered over her soft skin. There was nothing like being a parent. Nothing like watching her child grow and flourish.

Each milestone was bittersweet; they filled her with pride and relief, but also a sense of how quickly Maris was growing up. She'd already gingerly folded up the twelve-month-old clothes, held up each tiny shirt, and tucked it inside a cardboard box. The shimmery tulle dress Maris had worn to the wedding hung in the closet. She couldn't part with that one just yet. Damien and Lindsey had rented the room facing the sea at the restaurant where they shared a turbulent first date. They'd had a small winter ceremony with close family and friends, overlooking the ocean with the glow of flickering tea lights warming the room and the fragrance of creamy roses floating through the air.

Sand crunched behind her. Damien knelt down, moved her hair to one side, and placed a kiss against her jawline. A shiver ran down her spine as he whispered a playful suggestion in her ear. They both turned to Maris who was yelling "Shell!" A large toffee-colored conch had been tossed in her lap by a crashing wave.

"Wow, Maris!" Lindsey mirrored her daughter's excitement. "Hang on to that shell really tight. The most special treasures are washed in with the tide." A grin stretched over her face and she glanced at Damien who was smiling down at her.

He pulled her close. "They certainly are." His lips hovered just above hers and his breath tickled her skin. Goose bumps popped over her arms when he kissed her long and deep. This was the life she'd always dreamed of, the man she'd always wanted, and the family she cherished. She'd found it all on the Cape where she grew up, in the cottage by the sea.

The End

More great stories from Tule Publishing

Then Came You by Jeannie Moon

His Best Mistake by Lucy King

Something Old by Megan Ryder

Available now at your favorite online retailer!

About the Author

Contemporary Romance Author Charlee James was introduced to a life-long love of reading listening to her parents recite nightly stories to her and her older sister. Inspired by the incredible imaginations of authors like Bill Peet, Charlee could often be found crafting her own tales. As a teenager, she got her hands on a romance novel and was instantly hooked by the genre.

After graduating from Johnson & Wales University, her early career as a wedding planner gave her first-hand experience with couples who had gone the distance for love. Always fascinated by family dynamics, Charlee began writing heartwarming novels with happily-ever-afters.

Charlee is a New England native who lives with her husband, daughter, two rambunctious dogs, a cat, and numerous reptiles. When she's not spending time with her tight-knit family, she enjoys curling up with a book, practicing yoga, and collecting Boston Terrier knick-knacks.

Thank you for reading

In with the Tide

If you enjoyed this book, you can find more from all our great authors at TulePublishing.com, or from your favorite online retailer.

TULE
PUBLISHING

Made in the USA
Coppell, TX
28 October 2022

85316923R10132